SIMPLY YOU

MAGGIE WILD

For Tom and Barbara

IT RAINED on Sarah's wedding day. As luck would have it, she wasn't getting married.

Instead, she was slogging her bike up a steep country lane, the wind blowing her toward every pothole and puddle, the cold "British summer" rain lashing against her pink thighs.

"Come on, Cecelia," she muttered to her bike for about the twentieth time that day. "Don't stop, don't stop." But Cecelia only wobbled, threatening to pitch Sarah into a very muddy ditch.

More than once, she'd thought about sheltering in a warm country pub. She pictured sitting by a roaring fire, ordering a comforting lunch of hot mushroom soup and a wedge of crusty bread, washed down with a pint of Guinness. A taxi had whooshed past her about ten miles back and she'd had to stop herself from flagging it down and begging the driver to strap Cecelia to the roof and take them both somewhere warm and dry. At her lowest point, she'd entertained the idea of calling her fiancé and begging him to drive the three-plus hours up from London—or even send one of his staff—to collect her.

"In other words, be rescued," she muttered to herself, and there was no way she was going to do that. She needed this time to think, to make the right decision for herself, and she couldn't do that if, every time she snapped her fingers, Amir made everything perfect.

She pushed on toward the crest of the hill, changing her chant to "I think I can; I think I can." At least she hoped it was the crest. It was hard to tell if what she could see was the horizon or just the next band of thick, gray cloud, bringing another drenching of rain.

"Next time we do a long-distance bike tour," she gasped to Cecelia, "remind me to pick somewhere sunny."

Cecelia didn't respond. Sarah dug into the hill and recalled other trips she and her beloved bike had taken, pictured herself freewheeling down a sun-dappled lane in Tuscany or pedaling to baguettes and cheese on the patio of a Loire Valley cafe. She pictured Amir alongside her, his long lean legs matching her cadence, his chiseled features melting into the relaxed laugh she loved but didn't see enough.

The image disappeared in a damp cloud. She'd floated the idea of riding through Tuscany for their honeymoon, even though she knew that the last thing on Amir's list of relaxing ways to spend his time would be pedaling a bike through the countryside. Cruising through the Med on a chartered yacht or lounging on the sundeck of their private suite at a Hillingham hotel—perhaps in St. John or Bali or Bora Bora—was more Amir's idea of a good time. As much as she had relished the solitude of riding Cecelia through the countryside for the past week, at that exact moment in time, she might have traded it for a Pina Colada by the pool in Antigua.

The rain eased off as Sarah reached the brow of the hill, and the clouds lifted, as if someone had raised a theater curtain to reveal the stage. And what a stage they had set for her. The lane wound on a gentle decline through a vast expanse of parkland. A magnificent oak tree mushroomed in the distance, the grass around it dotted with lithe brown deer. Beyond, a lazy river eased its way under an arched stone bridge, kissing the overhanging branches of a weeping willow tree. And in the distance, surveying the entire scene like the lord of the manor, was an impressive country home.

Even the photographer's artistic shots of Atherton Hall, one of the Hillingham Group's "country retreats" and the property that had launched Amir's family's empire, didn't do the place justice. The dark stone of the massive house was punctuated by three rows of tall windows, each opening onto a veranda. The grand front entrance boasted marble columns leading up a flight of stone steps. To one side, a tall hedge concealed the hotel's most advertised feature—a secret garden, acres of carefully designed nooks offering guests peace, privacy, and most of all, luxury. When she'd told Amir she needed some time away to think, this had been his gift to her, his one concession to a trip he'd otherwise opposed. Two nights in the middle of her journey to rest, eat, sleep, and be pampered.

It still boggled Sarah's mind that this had once been the Hillingham family home, that Amir's great-grandmother had lived here as a girl, and had the foresight, as a young woman, to take in paying guests to save the family from poverty. Even Amir's mother, the reigning queen of Hillingham Hotels, still lived in the London home where Amir had grown up. Sarah had never lived anywhere for longer than two years. The first time she'd met Amir's family, she'd felt grounded and safe, a sense of belonging she'd never experienced before. She'd looked forward to becoming part of Amir's family, to tangling her shallow roots with his deep ones, but the wedding... the wedding had, well... the wedding had gotten away from her, out of control. Calling it off had been Sarah's doing. Amir had been supportive, not exactly happy, but at least understanding. She had told him over and over that she wasn't saying no to the marriage—she'd have to be an idiot to say no to the marriage—she was simply putting her foot down about what was turning out to be the wedding from hell.

Sarah pedaled hard, as if she could out-pedal the memories of telling Amir about her change of heart, and of breaking the news to his mother. She tried to fill her head with images from the hotel's brochure. By the time she rumbled Cecelia over the cattle grid at the end of the hotel's long driveway, she could almost feel the embracing waters of her first hot bath in days, pictured sliding into the gently scented bliss of bubbles and heat. She could imagine how it would feel to slip between thousand-count Egyptian cotton sheets and slumber under the caress of a goose down comforter without a worry in the world. She'd order breakfast in bed and read magazines until she was summoned to the spa for her appointments. Amir had set her up with a Serenity Package and for six hours a team of technicians would soak, scrub, exfoliate, wrap, oil, pummel, pinch, tweak, soothe, and otherwise pamper her to within an inch of her life. She sent a silent thank you to Amir and pedaled toward her haven.

Cecelia's tires crunched up the gravel driveway, slowing Sarah to a dangerously wobbly crawl. She unclipped her cycling shoes—once white with a stripe of metallic pink, but now a black mess of spotted mud, a pattern, she noticed to her dismay, that continued all the way up her legs—and dismounted. She leaned Cecelia against a column and stepped onto the long red welcome mat emblazoned with the gold Hillingham *Fleur de Lis*. For a moment, she hesitated outside the front entrance and took stock of her damp cycling clothes and the faint aroma of stale perspiration wafting up from her body. Her hair hung in a long, tangled ponytail, sweaty tendrils sticking to her face. If her legs were any indication, she knew she'd be wearing the cyclist's mark of distinction on her back—a spray of mud kicked up from her back tire and spattered in a fountain from the point where her bottom touched the saddle all the way up her back. Not attractive.

There was a time when stepping into an establishment like this would have intimidated Sarah, made her sure people could tell just by looking at her that she didn't belong, that she couldn't afford to be here. She always took care to dress the part when she was out with Amir, to make sure that she looked, from the outside, as if she belonged, even if on the inside she felt like a fraud. Well, now she looked like something the cat might drag in. In fact, she was such a mess, even the cat would take a wide berth around her. Every instinct told her not to go in. "Just turn around and walk away, Sarah," the little voice in her head hissed. "You don't belong here. You're not good enough. You're not the kind of person who comes to a place like this." All that was true, or it used to be, but not anymore.

"No," she whispered, aware that she'd moved beyond talking to herself and was arguing with herself out loud now. "You are Sarah Tildon, soon-to-be Sarah Tildon Hillingham. You are Amir's fiancée and you *do* belong."

With that, she squared her cold, damp shoulders and reached for the brass handle of the front door.

"Miss, Miss. Excuse me, Miss."

Sarah turned to see a young man hurrying toward her under the shelter of a black Hillingham Group golf umbrella. His stylish narrow-legged suit, slicked dark hair, and thick-framed designer glasses screamed authority and self-control, but the look on his face was panicked. "Stop!" he yelled, screeching to a halt a short distance from Sarah. "You can't go in there!"

The blood drained from Sarah's face and in the pit of her stomach came that old familiar feeling. *I've been caught. He knows about me.* She took a step backward away from the door, dropping her eyes so as not to let the man see her utter humiliation.

"I'm sorry, Miss," he said. "Could you come with me?"

Shame burned in Sarah's cheeks and the instinct to run twitched in her tired legs.

"Miss Tildon?" the man said, panic rising in his voice. "Please?"

Sarah jerked her head up at the sound of her name. So he did know who she was. He wasn't trying to throw her out, but he was trying to take her through a back entrance, so the other hotel guests wouldn't see her. That was almost as bad.

She felt sorry for the man having to do this unpleasant task. God knows she'd worked enough crappy jobs in her life and been stuck with the tasks no one else wanted to do.

She softened her expression. "Guillaume?" she said, reading from the man's name tag. "I'm really damp and really cold and the thing I'd love more than anything else in the world right now is a cup of tea and a hot bath. I know I'm a mess, but if you could just get me checked in, I promise you I clean up well." She flashed him a winning smile, but Guillaume seemed unfazed.

"Your attire isn't the problem, Miss Tildon," he said. "The bath is the problem. In fact, water in general is, I would say, our big problem at the moment."

Just then the sound of a motor juddering into action caused the tall windows to rattle. Sarah frowned.

"We've had a minor incident," said Guillaume. "A bit of a flood, actually. In the foyer. And the kitchens. And consequently the spa. We don't currently have a water supply. Or a power supply. So..."

Sarah felt like a polar bear, perched on a rapidly shrinking island of ice, watching her dreams drift away. The bath, the bed, the decadent dinner she'd envisioned for the past fifteen frigid miles, all faded away. She needed to be warm and dry and fed and asleep, but she wasn't going to be any of those things just yet. She felt an old familiar exhaustion wash over her and the deep, piercing fear of not knowing where she would sleep tonight. "We won't stay where we're not wanted," her mother would always say. Sarah blinked away the tears that prickled the rims of her eyes, and shook off the gloom. She wasn't being turned away; she was simply being rerouted. Not the same thing at all.

"I wish you'd let me know sooner. I could have made other plans."

"We did try to contact you. I left several messages. We've made arrangements to accommodate all our guests at other properties, but I couldn't reach you. I'm sorry you had to ride all this way in this awful weather."

Sarah's heart sank again as she pictured her phone stuffed deep inside her packed bike panniers, safe from the rain, and apparently out of earshot. Now, she was going to have to get back on her bike, back out in the rain.

"How far is the other place?" She pictured another hour, maybe two, shivering in the cold and wet.

"Twenty minutes or so by car," Guillaume said. "Mr. Hillingham requested we provide transportation for you and your trusty steed. We'll have a van arriving shortly."

Of course he did, she thought. Amir could move mountains with the flick of a finger. She'd seen entire guest suites reconfigured to suit a picky celebrity and lavish summer wedding receptions moved indoors with the threat of rain. She'd also seen him negotiate contracts and budge stalwart development committees over to his way of thinking, only for the defeated to share a drink and a laugh with him that same evening. Amir was used to people falling in with his plans. "You'll get used to it," his brother's wife had told Sarah. But Sarah was used to her independence; she'd no choice but to take care of herself growing up. She'd fallen in with Amir's plans for the wedding, and look where that had ended. If their marriage had a chance of making it, she had to stick up for herself. Starting now.

"There's a village close by, isn't there?" she asked. She'd passed a sign somewhere on the dreaded hill, but she couldn't for the life of her recall the name.

"Hope," said Guillaume. "Just a couple of miles from here."

"Do they have a hotel? A pub? Anything?"

"There's a bed & breakfast. I've heard good things, but it's certainly not up to Hillingham standards, and Mr. Hillingham would be very upset..."

"Mr. Hillingham will be fine. I'll deal with him. But if you could make a call and see if they have a room there, I'll make sure Mr. Hillingham hears how helpful you've been."

Guillaume hesitated and Sarah could see him weighing the needs of his guest with the expectations of his boss, or rather his boss's boss's boss. Finally, he cracked. "Come with me," he said.

Sarah followed him through a service door and down a narrow corridor to a small, neat office. Guillaume offered her a seat, but given the mud she knew was stuck to her, she declined to sit. While Guillaume looked for the phone number and placed a call, Sarah slumped against the desk, hugging her arms around her chest to stay warm. Amir wouldn't understand, of course, but at this point, she was fairly certain he had given up trying to understand the woman he planned to marry. Sometimes she wasn't entirely sure she understood herself. Falling in love with someone like Amir was complicated. In the business world, the Hillinghams were royalty, and Sarah was very much a commoner. But she loved that Amir used his family name to enable real change for the causes he was passionate about. And he loved her exactly because she was down-to-earth. Their marriage was founded on mutual admiration and not good business sense... much to his mother's disappointment. Still, Sarah knew people gossiped about her, said she was a gold digger, wondered what someone like Amir saw in someone like her. And even though she knew better than to let the rumors get to her, she was determined to prove that Sarah Tildon could take care of herself.

Now, her stubbornness had cost her a weekend of luxury, just like it had cost her a fairytale wedding. Instead, she was back off into the unknown, to a B&B in the middle of nowhere, the threat of a lumpy bed and a greasy breakfast trampling her visions of crisp sheets and a steaming lavender-scented bath.

She was about to tell Guillaume to hang up the phone

and call for transportation to another Hillingham hotel, when her gaze fell on a portrait hanging on the back wall of the office. From the middle of an overelaborate gold frame the cool eyes of Claudette Hillingham stared down at her. In two dimensional oil on canvas, Amir's mother looked even more formidable than in real life, if that were possible. She seemed to dare Sarah to defy her, to once again thwart her plans and forge her own path. She'd been furious about the wedding and she'd be furious if Sarah didn't fall into line again. But Sarah knew that if she gave in to Claudette once, she'd be giving in to her for the rest of her life. Despite the two nights of luxury she'd be giving up, she had to do this ride without Amir's help or Claudette's interference. She had to remind herself that, even if she married Amir—and by extension, married the Hillingham family—she was still more than capable of standing on her own two feet.

"Good news," said Guillaume, a big smile on his face. "There's a room with a bath booked for you for two nights and a request to have a tea tray waiting." He handed Sarah a bright yellow business card. On it was an illustration of a sunflower and the words "Sunnydale Bed & Breakfast, Hope Valley" in a friendly orange script. "And if you change your mind at any time, please don't hesitate to call me and I'll make it my personal mission to accommodate you elsewhere."

"Thank you, Guillaume," she said, giving Claudette's portrait a last triumphant glance before she turned and left. "And good luck."

With thoughts of homemade scones and a cozy room nestling in her imagination, Sarah eased herself gingerly back into Cecelia's saddle and turned in the direction of Hope Valley and the Sunnydale Bed & Breakfast.

CHAPTER TWO

SIX EGGS. Six measly eggs.

"Ladies," Michael said to the cluster of chickens scratching around at his feet. "I could use some help, if you don't mind. What will it take to get a few more eggs, eh?" By way of response, a fat black-and-white speckled hen clucked, fluffed her feathers, and pecked at the toe of Michael's work boot. "Watch it, Beatrice," he said, "or I'll put you in the pot."

The chicken looked at him, cocked her head, and pecked his boot again. Michael sighed as he gathered the basket of eggs to his chest and closed the door of the chicken coop behind him. His chickens knew he was a soft touch. Even if he hadn't gone against the advice of everyone he knew and given his girls names, they'd never see the inside of a stew pot, and they knew it.

Trouble was, this self-sufficient lifestyle relied on trading what he needed for what he produced, and six little eggs didn't give him much to barter with. An image popped into his mind of Caroline's face, that pitying look she'd give him when he failed at his dream of a simpler life. Perhaps he could hire her to give that same look to his chickens, guilt them into laying. But Caroline wouldn't settle for being paid in eggs. Especially not now she was marrying an accountant. How would "Mr. Dotted I's and Crossed T's" classify eggs on his profit and loss spreadsheet?

Michael pushed the image of his smug ex-fiancée and her pompous husband-to-be from his mind. He'd been in a grumpy mood all week, ever since she'd called with the news of her impending nuptials. She was history and he didn't need her—or anyone else—to live the life he'd always dreamed of. He transferred the six eggs to an egg box designed for a dozen. The six empty cardboard cups glared up at him like round laughing mouths. He sucked up his pride and pushed open the garden gate.

Yesterday's downpour had been welcome after an unusually dry start to the summer. The zucchini would be happy. The sky was that special clear blue that comes only after a good rain. He took a deep breath. He so rarely got to appreciate days like this anymore. He spent so much of his time looking down at the ground—plucking weeds, planting seeds, coaxing seedlings into plants, and cajoling chickens to lay eggs—that he seldom appreciated the surroundings of the place he'd been born and the place he'd chosen to come back to.

He stood for a moment and listened, shut out the nagging voice in his head that told him he didn't have time for frivolities when there was so much work to be done. He let the sound of the wind in the trees swirl around him, a clatter of crows cawing in the nearby woods, the faint hum of a tractor somewhere in the fields. He stretched his arms above his head, feeling a release in the tight muscles in his chest. He'd tilled a large bed for potatoes yesterday and the resulting soreness made him feel strangely alive. The village was so different from London and its constant thrum. Traffic, crowds, trains, taxis honking, busses spewing fumes, people elbowing, bustling, always hurrying somewhere. He didn't miss that at all.

His colleagues in The City had thought he was an idiot to leave, to turn his back on a thriving career, to give up the security of a ludicrous paycheck that had afforded him a very comfortable life. But his friends, his *real* friends, understood when he'd told them he wanted a simpler life. They knew how The City sucked the life out of a person, because their lives had been sucked out, too. In some ways they'd admired his decision to return to his roots and move back to Hope, but they all had more sense than to actually give up all they'd worked for.

He cut down a narrow cobbled alley that led to the back of his sister Nicki's B&B, and smelled sizzling bacon before his hand even touched the gate. He followed the scent through the neat back garden, his deprived senses picking up freshly baked muffins, toasted bread, and dark French-pressed coffee. His stomach growled, but he shook off the feeling and fixed a cheery grin on his face.

"Morning!" he said, as he pushed open the back door. The kitchen was a whirl of people, sounds, and smells, but as always, under Nicki's management, it looked like a perfectly coordinated ballet. Jennie, the student Nicki had taken on for the busy summer months, was juggling pans of eggs made to order—fried, poached, scrambled, and hard-boiled. She looked up as Michael came in and grinned wickedly. "Hello, gorgeous."

"You still here?" Michael said.

"Just so I can see you every morning."

It was the same banter they had every morning, but Michael didn't feel like laughing today.

He ignored the plate of bacon with its tantalizing tongues of deliciousness. There were sautéed mushrooms, fried tomatoes, baked beans, and even spotted rounds of black pudding, all made with the best local ingredients. In a cast iron pan that had once belonged to their great grandmother, Nicki had created a frittata, with yellow squash blossoms nestled in fluffy eggs and sprinkled with a snowfall of creamy feta cheese. Michael's mouth watered. He slid the eggs onto the counter and helped himself to a cup of tea from the big china pot Nicki always kept filled, trying not to let his gaze linger on the freshly baked scones.

"What you got for me?" his sister said, catching two slices of toast mid-air as they sprang from the toaster, cutting then into triangles and dropping them into a toast rack in one fluid movement.

"Half a dozen," said Michael. "Sorry."

Nicki glanced his way, her round face twisting quickly into a concerned expression. "Still not laying?"

Michael shook his head.

"And no idea why?"

Michael had consulted several sources of chicken expertise, but none of the explanations for eggless chickens seemed to fit his situation. His hens weren't old, he hadn't changed their food, and he wasn't aware of any trauma or worry. Even though the British summer had so far been typically damp, it hadn't been so bad that his chickens would be too cold to lay. Ever since he'd learned that Caroline was marrying his former friend, his feathered staff had rebelled and refused to lay. It was just a coincidence, but blaming Caroline somehow made him feel better.

The trouble was, he depended on his chickens. He and Nicki had developed an unofficial method of barter. Every day he brought her two dozen eggs, two pints of goat milk, and vegetables to feed her hungry bed-and-breakfast guests. In return she traded something he needed: a loaf of home-made bread, a box of teabags, the use of her washing machine, breakfast. In the off-season, when tourist business was quiet, she paid him back by helping him preserve his excess vegetables, making vats of tomato sauce, pickling beetroot, and creating outrageously delicious chutneys. She took some for herself and the rest Michael traded or sold to buy the things he couldn't grow or build. It had been a year since he'd committed to this self-sufficient lifestyle and, until his chickens had mutinied, it had all been working out well. Now, he wasn't so sure.

"Try not to worry," said Nicki, her voice softening the way their mother's did when they got scrapes as children. She handed him a plate of frittata with a side of plump rasp-berries and tiny alpine strawberries. "You can earn your breakfast by serving this to table three. We'll sort out your rebellious chickens later."

Michael took the plate, grateful to Nicki for not trying to offer a free breakfast. He had a hard and fast rule about his charity: he'd accept gifts on his birthday and Christmas, but anything else he took from others, whether that was help planting potatoes, a homemade rhubarb pie (his soft spot), or breakfast from Nicki, had to be paid for in trade of goods or labor. It wasn't stubbornness that kept him from accepting help, nor was it a lack of money. It was the prin-ciple of the thing. He'd set out to prove he could make this way of life work and he was determined to do it his way.

"Just a minute," said Nicki. She stepped over and plucked a stray chicken feather from his hair and straight-ened the collar of his denim shirt. Nicki's B&B, Sunnydale, attracted hikers, mountain bikers, and general down-to-earth outdoorsy sorts who wouldn't be offended if their breakfast waiter was a tad scruffy. But occasionally, guests drove in for a weekend in the country, looking for the charm of a quaint cottage without the hassle of cooking for themselves. Michael knew those sorts; he'd worked with plenty of them in The City, and he knew they wouldn't appreciate their breakfast served with a side of chicken feather and essence of goat.

Nicki gave him a quick sniff and pinched his cheek. "Got to make sure you're presentable for my guests," she said, standing back and giving him an appraising once-over. Jennie leaned in and let her eyes run over him.

"What do you think?" Nicki asked her.

Jennie pretended to be unimpressed. "Not bad I suppose. He'd fetch a couple of quid at market." She gave his bicep a quick squeeze, as if assessing livestock at the Monday market. Michael gave her a provocative smile. He had always kept himself in shape, but while those early morning runs through Regent's Park and the evening tours of the weight room at the gym had kept his desk-bound body trim and toned in London, this new line of work had made him... "Brawny," Jennie said.

He laughed at the word, conjuring images of broad-chinned lumberjacks. But he had to admit it was fitting. Manual labor looked good on him.

"Table three looks hungry," Nicki said, causing Michael to turn and look. "Not for you, Romeo. For my frittata."

Michael fumbled the plate and hurried into the dining room. Behind him Nicki cackled, a laugh that rumbled from deep inside her and was loud enough to crack cement.

Michael shook his head. *His crazy sister.*

Michael couldn't tell at first glance whether the woman sitting alone at the small table by the window was the outdoor type or the city type. She was tall and slender, with lean tanned limbs that suggested time outdoors. She wore a pale cotton skirt and a simple white t-shirt, nothing dressy. But, as he got closer, he could see she hadn't just pulled on the nearest clothes from the top of a backpack. Her t-shirt fitted as if it had been tailored, and her long, butter and toast-colored hair hung in a glossy veil over one shoulder. This wasn't a woman dressed for a day in the mud; this was a woman who'd thought out her wardrobe, probably thought out every detail of her life. He didn't like to use labels but if this woman wasn't "high maintenance," she was certainly highly maintained.

He glanced at the plate. Egg-white frittata, no cheese, fruit, no potatoes. Definitely H.M.

"One frittata, freshly made with local eggs," he said, sliding the plate onto the table. He would have liked to have added that they were fresh-laid that morning, but his bolshy brood had seen to that.

The woman turned his way and flashed him a gentle smile. It lit up her face, which was heart-shaped, with wide cheekbones curving to a small pointy chin, but the smile didn't reach her eyes. Beautiful, but sad, he thought. Still, something inside him stirred when she smiled. Actually, something *outside* him stirred and he shifted his weight and focused his gaze on the frittata instead. Getting up pre-dawn and working all day tending chickens and mucking about in the dirt hadn't left much time for thoughts of the flesh, and he was glad to realize he wasn't dead, just dead tired.

The woman's warm dark eyes peered up at him from behind her curtain of hair and her smooth plummy lips curled into an enticing smile. She had freckles dappled across her nose, and as her smile widened, two small, crescent-moon dimples folded at the edges of her cheeks.

"From your chickens?" she said, taking the plate from him. "You're a farmer?"

She had a warm voice that curled around her vowels, but underneath he detected a hint of roughness, an accent he couldn't pin down to a single place. Wherever it was from originally, she'd worked hard to cover it up.

"Not exactly a farmer," he said. "I have a small holding, some chickens and goats. I bring fresh eggs for my sister; she gives me a good breakfast in return."

"You grow your own food, as well?"

"Pretty much everything I eat I grow, trade the rest."

The woman raised her eyebrows. It was a typical reaction when he told people about his lifestyle. First they were shocked, and then they'd say how nice it would be to live a simple life like that. And then they'd get into their fancy cars and go back to their houses and jobs and mortgages. And maybe now and then they'd wish their lives were simpler, but they'd never make the leap. On days like today, even Michael doubted his decision to downsize.

"Sounds like a lovely life," the woman said, getting that faraway dreamy look.

Michael waited for her to thud back to his reality.

"Must be challenging though. A bit stressful, I imagine," she said.

"Well, today my chickens are acting up and yesterday the rabbits found a way under my formerly rabbit-proof fence and made light work of half my cabbages." *And my water heater is on the fritz, and my van needs a service, and some days I dream about lying on the beach with the Mediterranean sun warming my body with the woman of my dreams beside me.* But he didn't share those details with the woman. "But I wouldn't change it for anything." That bit was true.

As she adjusted her plate to admire the frittata, her teaspoon tumbled to the floor and Michael reached to retrieve it. His gaze followed her long, smooth legs down from the hem of her skirt to the floor. Her tan stopped at a perfectly straight line just below her ankle. Below it was a strip of creamy white skin. He recognized immediately the tell-tale sock line of someone who spent a lot of time outdoors. For a brief moment he thought how nice it would be to abandon his moody chickens to fend for themselves and spend the day rambling through the hills in her company.

"Rain cleared out nicely," she said.

"Got big plans for the day?"

"Actually, I don't," she laughed. "I'm in the unusual situation of having my plans completely upended, but to tell you the truth I'm looking forward to spending a day ambling around and exploring."

"I thought you might be hiking today."

"That's about the last thing my legs would appreciate today. I came in on my bike yesterday."

"In that rain?"

"In that rain."

"Hope you didn't ride far."

That laugh again. On anyone else he would have been sure she was mocking him, but her eyes sparkled and her face glowed and he guessed she was just one of those people who laughed easily. "Actually, I've ridden from London. Not in one day, of course. It's taken me a week to get this far, and I'm about halfway."

"You're riding to Scotland?"

"Edinburgh. That's the plan," she said.

He glanced at her legs again. Cyclist's legs. That explained a lot. London to Edinburgh. What was that? Four hundred miles? Four-and-a-half hours by train, seven by car, and two weeks by bike, apparently. He shook his head. Whatever possessed someone to get on a bike and ride the entire length of the country? He'd never understand it, but there you go. Everyone has their own definition of madness.

"You must be mad," he said out loud, before he could stop himself.

"Says the man who relies on stubborn chickens and can't even outwit a rabbit." That laugh again. It made her whole face glow. He pictured the woman sitting in the corner of his couch, her feet tucked up underneath her, a glass of his homemade wine in her hand, laughing as he told her stories. Yes, his couch was lumpy and sagged in the middle, but someone who could ride two hundred miles in the British weather and still share a laugh over breakfast was not the high maintenance sort he'd first imagined.

"Believe me," she said, "you're not the first person to call me mad. After yesterday I'm starting to wonder if you're right."

"Well," said Michael, "I wish you the very best of luck. And if you need any ideas of how to fill your day, don't hesitate to ask. My place is at the end of the village; you'll have ridden right past it last night. I'm Nicki's big brother." He held out his hand. "Michael."

She smiled that dazzling smile again and it made him feel almost faint. "Sarah," she said, holding out her hand to shake his. And that's when he saw the ring.

In post-game analysis, or whatever they called it, Michael had made a fool of himself. He'd called out Sarah as high-maintenance at first glance, so why hadn't he listened to his instincts? It wasn't anything she'd said or done. She'd been perfectly nice in that regard, but then that ring. The ring told him everything he needed to know.

Michael had a vast wealth of experience with engagement rings. Oh, my goodness, hadn't he just. He'd spent so much time sneaking around Caroline's friends, getting opinions about the perfect ring, that he'd almost blown the entire proposal. Caroline had as good as accused him of having an affair, even as he'd dropped to one knee to ask her to marry him. Ironic that infidelity had been her biggest worry, when she'd turned out to be an expert on the subject. She'd oohed and aahed over the ring and told him it was beautiful, even had tears in her eyes, but hint by hint she'd let him know it wasn't quite up to her standards. In the end she'd designed the ring herself, chosen the jeweler, insisted on a second opinion on the quality of the stone, and Michael had almost had to take out a second mortgage to pay for it. Some people had told him that the cost of the wedding was inversely proportional to the length of the marriage, but Michael just appreciated Caroline's class. Unfortunately, that class didn't extend to loyalty. Caroline had returned the ring—although Michael was now stuck with the thing—and Michael had been left to lick his wounds in the peace of his childhood home.

But the rock on Sarah's finger had been, well astronomical. Quite literally she had a small asteroid perched on a silver band (silver-colored; he had no doubt it would be platinum, expert that he was). It was a wonder she could lift her finger.

Well, she'd provided a pleasant distraction to his morning, but now he had to get back to his chickens. Waiting on one table wouldn't be enough to cover his end of the trade with Nicki. He needed to get his act together and he needed to do it soon. Because if there was anything Michael refused to do, it was to rely on someone else for help.

CHAPTER THREE

AFTER BREAKFAST, that delicious frittata made with Michael's home-produced eggs, Sarah weighed her options for how to spend the rest of her day. It was amazing how a good night's sleep in a comfy bed had changed her whole attitude. She'd arrived at Sunnydale cold and damp on the afternoon of The Wedding that Wasn't. Nicki had met her at the gate and shown her to the shed where she could lock up Cecelia. Sarah had secured the lock and almost cried when she realized her combination was her wedding date and now she'd have to change it. Nicki had ushered her into the warmth of the B&B and shown Sarah to her room on the top floor, apologizing for all the stairs. Sarah had waved off the apology, even as her legs had protested at every step. But the room was spacious and well appointed. There was a high bed piled with thick fluffy quilts and pillows, and a small settee that looked out over the neat backyard. Best of all was the deep claw-foot tub that had been set below a corner window so Sarah could watch the birds flit past as she soaked up to her chin in bubbles. She'd unpacked some clothes to let the creases drop out, and drawn a bath to soak out her muscle aches. She was already wrapped in the yellow fluffy dressing gown she'd found folded at the foot of the bed when Nicki knocked at her door again bearing a tray of tea, freshly baked scones and a ramekin of home-made raspberry jam. Sarah had taken it into the bathroom and devoured the entire thing while sitting in the bath. She'd hobbled to the local pub for an early dinner and collapsed into bed before dusk. She couldn't recall hearing a single sound until the church bells chiming seven in the morning woke her.

Now she was rested and fed, she considered ringing Amir to let him know where she'd ended up spending the night. He would certainly have heard from Guillaume that she'd decided not to take him up on the alternative accommodations. They'd instituted a policy before she'd left, or rather she'd instituted the policy and he'd agreed: She would check in with him via text every night to let him know she was okay, but he wasn't to call her unless there was an emergency. So far, he'd adhered to the policy, although she had to admit that she wished he missed her enough to break the rule. But this was supposed to be her time to think, to push her personal reset, and shake off some of the stress from planning what was very nearly The Wedding From Hell. So much of her life had gone off track lately, and she needed this couple of weeks under her own steam to get everything back under control. What she needed today was a gentle walk in the countryside and space in her head to let her thoughts sort themselves out.

It was a postcard-perfect day and Sarah realized that, even traveling at the leisurely pace of ten or fifteen miles per hour on her bike, she missed so many details as she zipped along. The village, Hope, was charming. The main road cut down a long wide valley that arched up to a rugged ridge on one side and a long, angular skyline on the other, a network of footpaths crisscrossing along the hillside. Stone cottages flanked each side of the narrow road, with a post office, a row of shops, and the mandatory tea room clustered around a small village square. A banner announcing the Midsummer Fair the following weekend stretched across the street. It was a pity she'd miss the local festivities.

She glanced behind her to the bottom end of the village, the way she'd come in the night before. Just before the road turned and crossed the stone arch bridge over the river stood a two-story stone farmhouse. Was that where Michael lived? Her legs twitched as if urging her to go that way and see his place. She was curious to see how he lived. Her brain, thank goodness, had the upper hand. She turned away and continued through the village, passing the pub and a row of old stone cottages. In the front garden of the first one, an elderly woman was deadheading roses.

"Nice morning," Sarah said as she passed.

"My roses like the rain but I can't say I do," said the woman. She had a kind face and a cheery smile. She reminded Sarah of Grandma Lily. She'd spent a lot of summers at her grandmother's house and they were among her best memories. Only when she was older did she understand that she and her brother, Luke, had been dumped there while their mother dealt with the crisis *du jour*. After their dad left them for good when Sarah was eight, Grandma Lily's had become a sanctuary, the one place Sarah ever felt safe.

"Have a nice walk," the old lady said as Sarah passed. "And if you stop at the tea room on your way back, you shouldn't pass up their scones. Best I've ever had."

Sarah thanked the old lady and wondered if it would be weird if she took over a scone for her later. She would never take food to strangers in London, but here it felt right. As she reached the end of the garden wall, she heard the old lady singing to herself, just like Grandma Lily used to do. Or perhaps she wasn't singing to herself, but to her plants. Grandma Lily said singing made everything better. She sang to her grandchildren, her plants, her cats. Sarah had once even caught her leaning over the fence and singing to her neighbor's chickens. "Encourages them to lay," she'd told Sarah.

She was all the way to the signpost for the footpath up the hill when the penny finally dropped. She turned on her heel and hurried back through the village. She needed to get to Michael's house and tell him she might have the solution to his chicken problem. As she reached the old lady's cottage, she stopped. What was she going to do, walk up and tell him he should sing to his chickens? It sounded insane to Sarah even though she'd seen it done. If she saw him later, she could casually tell the story about her Grandma and leave him to decide if it was worth a try.

She turned and headed back to her walk route, but before she reached the stile, she changed her mind again. Maybe she'd walk casually past Michael's place, mention the story, and leave it at that. She'd love to see his garden, anyway, so that was that.

"Are you lost?" asked the old lady when Sarah passed for the third time.

It was a big question. She had been lost when she called off the wedding, torn between marrying the man she loved and feeling that her life was slipping out of her own control. When it was just the two of them, alone, life with Amir was perfect, but outside their bubble, Amir became the star of the show and Sarah felt like a bit player, taking the stage on cue, but never having any lines. Although she hated the term, she'd taken the bike trip in hopes of "finding herself." She had a brief thought that going out of her way to talk to a very attractive man about singing to his chickens didn't sound like finding herself, but she brushed aside the thought.

"No," she said to the old lady. "Just a little confused."

The woman smiled. "Well, you take your time, dear. You don't want to rush into things."

That was exactly what her Gran would have said, if she were still here.

When she reached the house she thought was Michael's, she peered over the garden wall to see a jeans-clad behind bending over a row of something green and edible. What, she couldn't tell, but as an avid vegetable lover, she was sure she'd recognize it if it turned up on her plate, carefully prepared by a discerning chef. She couldn't help but notice that Michael was very attractive from this angle. His body seemed solid, as if it could withstand all sorts of punishment in the hard work department.

She'd been surprised at first to learn that the man who'd served her breakfast was Nicki's brother. When Sarah had complimented Nicki's homemade raspberry jam the previous night, Nicki had mentioned that her brother grew the berries on his farm. Sarah had pictured a robust red-faced man with a large belly protruding from the opening in his tweed jacket. Michael didn't fit that image at all. He was a darker, taller, more rugged version of his sister. Where Nicki's curls were light brown and tumbled out from the headscarf she wore to tame them, Michael's were almost black and spilled in shiny waves over the collar of his denim shirt. Where Nicki's body rolled in maternal curves, Michael was cut in a V from his broad shoulders to his square hips. Where Nicki's smile overflowed in hearty chortles, Michael's laugh hummed like a well-tuned engine in his chest.

"Hello," she called, wondering immediately if the polite thing to do might have been to leave him to his work.

"Sarah," he said, straightening up and stretching his back. He remembered her name. She liked that.

"You look busy," she said. Why did she always say stupid things like that? She was an intelligent woman. She had a degree in biology and an MBA, for pity's sake, and she couldn't come up with anything more profound to say than, "You look busy."

But he smiled and ambled her way. "I never seem to run out of things to do around here and the amazing thing is, there are always more waiting for me the next day."

"Your garden's fabulous," she said. "Is it all vegetables?" Sarah herself loved a well-tended flower garden. When her Grandmother was still alive they'd gone together to the Chelsea Flower Show and spent the entire day wandering the grounds and admiring the displays. She'd love to have a garden of her own, but the best she could manage in London was a couple of flower boxes on the tiny balcony of her shared flat. But even those had suffered neglect during the wedding planning, and now she'd left them entirely. She doubted her flatmates would remember to water them, even though she'd asked.

"I don't have many flowers, unfortunately. Function over form in this case and unless they're edible, they're not much good to me," Michael said.

"This is a lot of veg for one person," she said, then clammed up at the assumption she'd just made. Of course he couldn't eat all this by himself. And why would he be by himself? Obviously there had to be a Mrs. Michael and a brood of little Michaels. She noted that he didn't wear a wedding ring, but perhaps that was a choice, given the amount of time he would have to spend with his hands in the dirt or ferreting around under chickens in search of eggs.

"I eat what I need and trade most of it."

I not *we*, Sarah noted.

"What do you trade for? If you don't mind me asking."

Michael's face crinkled into an amused smile. "You'd be amazed. I've traded for boots, tools, machinery parts. I've even traded for curtains. Basically, whatever money could buy I trade for instead."

"Oh," said Sarah, in another pointless response. She wasn't sure what to ask next that wouldn't come across as impolite. Her list of options were:

1. Why don't you just use money like normal people?

2. Is this a choice or are you just poor?

She couldn't quite decide how to frame the last question, but it was along the lines of:

3. Are you some sort of weirdo and if so, what sort?

"It, um, sounds like an interesting way to do things," she said, hoping that was a more appropriate thing to say.

Michael pulled off his work gloves and ran a hand through his thick, dark curls. A clump of mud detached itself from his sleeve and smeared itself across his cheek. Sarah found her fingers twitching to reach out and brush it off.

"I wish I could tell you I wouldn't have it any other way, but some days I wonder what I was thinking."

Sarah twitched her head to one side, still not able to frame a question, but hoping he'd take it upon himself to elaborate.

"Self-sufficiency, living off the land. It always sounded so romantic, you know? Not tied to a desk job, not answering to some corporate stiff, making your own rules and your own schedule."

"That does sound heavenly." When she'd first volunteered at the wildlife rescue sanctuary as a student, one of her roles was to capture the injured animals that people called to report. She'd loved jaunting around the countryside in her little van, stalking injured foxes in hedgerows, climbing into ditches to snag frightened rabbits. She'd thought about becoming a vet, but there was no money for more school, and the wildlife rescue people soon discovered she had a knack for grant writing and fundraising. She loved the work, not to mention it was how she'd met Amir. But every now and then, on her time off, she still volunteered to run rescue missions.

"If I'm going to be honest with you," Michael said. "It's a lot of work. I'd never admit it to my sisters, but there are days I miss the city."

"You're from London?"

"I'm from here originally, born and raised. But I went off to seek my fortune in the big city." He laughed to himself. "Life in the fast lane. And then one day I realized I'd had enough. Packed up my life in London and came home to this."

"Do you regret it?" she asked.

He paused for a moment longer than your average thinking time before he answered. "Nah. I love it. There are days that I don't love, but I don't regret coming back. This will always be home."

Sarah nodded like she understood, but she didn't really. If she decided to go "home," she'd have no idea where that would be. Amir's flat in Chelsea had been her part-time home for the past year or so, a big step up from the cramped flat in Clapham she shared with an ICU nurse and a museum archivist. But if she had to go back to her roots, she wouldn't know where to look. The industrial suburbs of the Midlands, the cramped inner-city bedsits, the dull small town in the middle of nowhere? She'd moved so many times as a child she couldn't remember where she'd lived the longest. Perhaps the only place she'd ever considered home was Grandma Lily's narrow terrace house. She'd always felt at home there, but now even that was gone, and so was the one person who'd ever made her feel like family.

"Fancy a tour?" Michael said. He was already moving toward the peeling wooden gate and it was clear that he wasn't going to wait for an answer. Sarah glanced at her neat leather walking shoes and clean pink socks. Oh well, she thought, it's only dirt.

"If you're not too busy," she said, and stepped through the gate to follow Michael.

She wasn't sure she'd ever met anyone with so much enthusiasm for vegetables. He walked her down rows of beans, explaining the difference between French and Scarlet Runners. He pointed out vast swaths of dark green leaves and listed more varieties of potato than she knew existed. He explained to her the basics of crop rotation, how he switched around where he planted the different types of crop each year so as not to deplete certain nutrients. He pointed out a carpet of alfalfa, a cover crop whose purpose was to add nitrogen back into the soil. It had the added advantage, he told her, of also feeding his goats.

"Goats?" Sarah asked warily, but Michael only grinned. As he led her to an enclosure, she noticed the easy way he moved across his land, like a man completely at home in his environment. With the ease of a gymnast, he hopped a fence high enough that Sarah would have been nervous to climb.

"Good morning, ladies," he said as three goats all but galloped out to meet him. He scratched their heads and handed Sarah a carrot to feed them. "Meet Bertha, Lulabelle, and Daphne."

Sarah held out the carrots and flinched as a brown and white goat nudged the others aside to get to it. The goats were cute, but their long square teeth looked like they could deliver a painful nip.

"Want to meet my pride and joy?" Michael asked.

Sarah nodded, happy to leave the goats, and followed Michael toward a wooden shed at the edge of a small enclosure. Through the gaps in the covered windows, Sarah could see the warm glow of a deep orange light. As she stepped through the door that Michael held open for her, she felt a blanket of gentle heat wrap around her. The shed had a row of deep shelves, like a workbench, all around its wall. At intervals, lights that looked like the old-fashioned sun lamp her mother used to have were attached to the wall above enclosed boxes.

"Hear that?" Michael said, beaming at her like a little boy showing his spider collection.

Sarah held still and listened. She could hear high pitched beeps, as if Michael was storing piles of tech equipment all with low battery alarms going off. He reached into one of the boxes and Sarah fully expected him to hand her an obsolete cellphone, but when he opened his hands, he held the tiniest chick. It was black and gray with a little splash of white on its chest, and the top of its head was a mass of yellow fluff as if it was wearing a fuzzy mohair hat.

"What is it?" Sarah said, peering at the little creature that now peeped at her as if it was earnestly trying to tell her its (short) life story.

"It's called a Legbar," said Michael, and when Sarah looked confused, he added, "It's a chicken."

Now he'd said it, she could see that the stubby orange beak and the spindly feet were definitely chicken-like, but this little fellow looked nothing like the fluffy yellow chicks she associated with Easter.

"I have six different varieties and they all look different. Come and look at this one," he said, ducking down to another heated box on the floor.

Sarah crouched beside him. She could smell lavender laundry detergent and spicy soap along with a vague aroma of freshly turned earth. Underneath it all was the musky smell of hard-working man. It wasn't a scent she smelled much in her life of suits and ties, and she found herself breathing it in and letting it settle deep within her.

"I've nicknamed her Zorro," Michael said, beaming at Sarah as he placed the chick in her hands.

"Zorro" was pale yellow, like the chicks she was used to seeing, but the top of her head was speckled and, around her eyes and across her pinkish beak, she had a strip of black feathers, like a tiny mask.

Sarah resisted the urge to say how cute Zorro was, and failed. She held the chick up at eye level and found herself twittering baby talk at it.

Michael laughed. "Hard to resist, isn't she?"

Sarah had to agree she was. She tickled Zorro's head and felt the warmth radiating from her tiny body. "What are you going to do with them?" she asked, immediately wishing she hadn't. At the end of the day, she knew that Michael was a farmer, and she'd learned a long time ago that farmers couldn't afford to be sentimental. She handed Zorro back to Michael, already more attached than she wanted to be.

"To be honest," Michael said placing Zorro back in her box, "they're an asset—eggs, manure, plus they're great for keeping the bug population at bay."

"And meat?" Sarah asked, hesitantly. "Do you eat them?"

Michael sighed. "That was the plan. But none of the chicken books mention that they have personalities. With my first batch of chicks I made the mistake of naming them. I'd go out and greet them every morning and the more I talked to them the more eggs they seemed to produce. But now they're not laying and it's time for the pot."

He paused and Sarah tried to erase an image that was forming of Zorro surrounded by tiny carrots and herbs. But Michael shook his head. "I can't do it. How can I put Henrietta and Harriet on the table? So, now I have my pet chickens and my new chicks for eggs."

"Your new chicks, like Zorro?"

He nodded. "I don't know what to tell you. I've got a soft spot for chickens. And if that makes me a rotten self-sufficient farmer, so be it." He shrugged and patted Zorro on the head. Sarah couldn't help but smile at the big tough man and the chickens that had stolen his tender heart.

"If you don't mind me asking," Sarah said, "what on earth possessed you to make such a big change? I mean, I love the *idea* of this lifestyle. It seems so simple and..." she searched for the right word. "Real. But I could never make such a big step."

Michael didn't answer at first and when she turned to look at him, a dark shadow had passed across his face. "Oh, you know," he said, but she didn't know. "I did want a simpler life and it does feel more real. I thought there had to be something more to life than the rat race, that constant chasing after something bigger and better. I suppose I'm just old-fashioned at heart." He looked away and Sarah sensed there was more to the story, but he didn't look like he was going to tell. She had so many more questions, like how did he afford to keep up the house? How did he sleep at night with no money coming in? It wasn't that everything always had to be about money, but the reality was, there were times when good looks and a bold dream just wouldn't be enough. It did sound like a romantic life, but the reality was way too unpredictable for her. She'd have bags under her eyes the size of her bike panniers if she had to go to bed every night with no financial security. She knew exactly what it was like to live never knowing if there was enough money to pay the bills, always wondering when she'd have to move again. She swore she would never live that way again and she'd worked hard to support herself ever since.

Grandma Lily would have liked Michael, though. "Salt of the earth," she would have said. Which reminded Sarah of why she'd come to talk to Michael in the first place.

"Speaking of old-fashioned, I did stop by for a reason. I was thinking about something my Gran once did, and you're probably going to think I'm crazy, but maybe it could work for your chickens."

"At this point I'll try anything," Michael said.

"Well," said Sarah, "is there any chance you can sing?"

CHAPTER FOUR

TWO DAYS after The Wedding that Wasn't, the sound of birds twittering in the trees drifted into Sarah's consciousness. She shifted in the wide, soft bed, snuggling her head into the feathery pillow and pulling the quilt around her shoulders. She ran a hand over her belly, feeling the firmness of her abs beneath the softness of her skin. Her body felt different. She felt different. Relaxed, that was it. No wonder she didn't recognize it. It had been a long, long time since she'd felt this peaceful.

She'd been right to take this trip. She knew she needed time away. The sanctuary's last fundraiser hadn't quite raised the money to cover the medical supplies and new paid staff they needed. She'd be busier than ever when she got back. And the wedding—or at least the planning—had been stressful. It wasn't just the juggling of tasks and coordinating all the details that had worn her out; it was the underlying knowledge that the whole production wasn't even the wedding she truly wanted. She just wanted to marry Amir without the fanfare.

But now she was feeling like her old self and it was time

to hit the road again. One more week in the saddle and she'd be with Amir again. They'd celebrate her accomplishment of riding the length of the country and then they'd get down to the business of planning the wedding they really wanted, the one that was right for them.

So why didn't she feel like getting out of bed? She lay there a little longer, staring up at the pale sloping ceiling of her room. She'd only spent two nights and it already felt like home. She liked the simple decor, the sunny yellow walls, the classic wooden bedframe, the bright curtains. She loved the feel of the rug between her toes when she climbed out of bed. She liked the cool of the black and white tiles in the bathroom and the curve of the clawfoot tub. If she had her own little place in the country, this is what it would be like. Simple, clean, and cozy. The complete opposite of the stylish sleek feel of Amir's London flat, the place that would soon become her home.

The flat was amazing in one sense, spread over the top two floors of an Edwardian row house overlooking a quiet park, and an easy bike ride across the river to work. But the interior was pure hi-tech bachelor pad. Amir's designers had done an impeccable job and the flat wouldn't have looked out of place in a swanky architecture magazine. But it wasn't a place to be comfortable. It wasn't a place she could kick off her shoes and slough around in flannel pajamas and furry slippers. It was the kind of place that made you feel obligated to do your hair just to go to the bathroom.

"When you move in you can do whatever you like with it," Amir had told her. But Sarah's job had made her pragmatic about spending and there was no way she could throw out a chair that had cost more than she made in a month just because she didn't like how it looked.

She wondered what the inside of Michael's house was like. She pictured over-stuffed armchairs and rustic furniture, a big wooden four-poster bed and a rumpled handmade quilt.

"Right!" she said, and threw back the covers. "No need to go there." This village—and its occupants—were clouding her judgment. It was time to get back in the saddle, literally and figuratively. She swung her feet to the floor and nestled her toes into the rug for what would probably be the last time. It felt so good that she lingered a little longer. Then she took a shower and put on her bike gear. She took a last look at the view from the high window. It really was a pretty village. Perhaps she could come back sometime with Amir.

No, she thought. *This will be my place.*

She let her gaze drift over the little church and the village green. She wished she could have stayed for the Midsummer Festival, but by Friday she'd be halfway to the Scottish border. Maybe she'd find another village and join in their festivities. Nice, but it wouldn't be the same.

Sarah had a quick breakfast of grapefruit juice and cereals. When Jennie came to take her order, she asked for a single scrambled egg and toast. She would regret not fueling up a few miles into her ride, but she didn't want to stay around long enough for Michael to bring her eggs again. She would stop by on her way out and say a quick goodbye to him; no need to get sentimental. The quicker she was on her way the better off everyone would be.

She finished her coffee and settled up her bill with Nicki.

"I hope you've enjoyed your stay," Nicki said as she ran Sarah's card through the machine.

"I can honestly say this has been my favorite stop so far."

"Then you'll have to come back and see us again."

Nicki held Sarah's gaze for a moment longer than was comfortable. Sarah's face flushed as if she'd been caught with a secret. But she had no secrets from Nicki.

"I'd love to," Sarah said, pocketing the little card that Nicki handed her. Like she needed a card to remember this place. She'd have to pedal like a banshee to erase it from her mind.

Back in her room, she cleaned her teeth and packed the last of her kit into her panniers. She took a last look around the room and felt a pang of sadness to be leaving it. But it wasn't *her* room, she reminded herself, it was just a temporary room for rent, and tonight when she pulled into her next stopping point, someone else would be settling in here. She hoped they loved it as much as she had. She pushed aside the pang of jealousy and closed the door behind her.

It was cool outside, but she could already tell by the way the sun cut down the valley that it was going to be a gorgeous day. She'd need to get some miles behind her this morning before it got too hot. Oh, the British weather. It knew how to keep a girl on her toes.

She gave a last wave to Nicki through the open kitchen door and headed for the shed, her cleats scraping on the stone path like aggressive tap shoes. She dumped her panniers against the low wall and pulled open the shed door. Against the wall, where she'd left Cecelia two days earlier, was... nothing.

Sarah halted, one foot in the shed and the other out. Her heart began to thud in her chest. The bike was definitely not there. She swung the door all the way open to allow more light inside. Maybe someone had moved it. She searched the depths of the shed as her eyes adjusted, but Cecelia was most definitely not there. Cecelia, the bike that she had saved for, the first big purchase she had ever made with her own money, made unique with components she had added one by one over the years, adorned with the rusty bell she'd had since she was eight: All gone.

Keep calm, she told herself. There's going to be a good explanation for this. She hurried back to the kitchen, where Nicki was juggling four pans, as usual.

"Sorry to bother you," said Sarah, fighting to keep her voice level. "Has my bike been moved?" Even as she asked, she realized it was a stupid question. Why would Nicki move her bike without telling her? Plus, she distinctly remembered locking it, remembered thinking about the combination and her wedding date.

"It's in the shed," said Nicki.

Sarah shook her head.

"I saw it last night."

"Well, it's not there now."

Nicki and Jennie exchanged a look. "Keep an eye on these," Nicki said, handing the spatula to Jennie. She wiped her hands on a towel and led Sarah out to the shed.

"There," she said, flinging open the shed door. "It's right..." Her voice trailed off as she and Sarah stared at the blank wooden wall of the shed. "Oh my God!" she whispered, confirming what Sarah had known right away. Her beloved bike was gone. Someone had stolen Cecelia.

CHAPTER FIVE

MICHAEL COULDN'T WAIT to get to Nicki's. It had worked! Sarah's idea to sing to the chickens had done the trick and today he had a full dozen eggs for his sister. He was excited to show Nicki, but he was more excited to see Sarah and tell her. He hoped she hadn't already left.

Visitors trickled through Nicki's B&B like water in the little stream that curled through the bottom of the village. They came, they saw, they got back in their cars and went home to civilization. Why should Sarah be any different? And yet, he hoped she would come by, just to stick in her head to say goodbye to the chickens, if not to him. He thought they'd had a connection, but maybe he was wrong.

He shook his head, flinging his silly fantasies away. What exactly did he think she'd say? "Oh, yeah, it was really nice meeting you. Sorry I couldn't stay and kindle whatever romantic notions you're hatching, but hey, I'm getting *married!*"

And yet there'd been something about Sarah. It was something he was thinking about when he went to bed the previous night and something he was still thinking about when he woke up in the morning. It was the tender way she'd held Zorro, how she'd tramped through his muddy garden in her neat little shoes and pink socks, showing him the massive fissure in her high maintenance veneer. He knew what high maintenance looked like. The dictionary definition showed a picture of Caroline—her precise wardrobe of clothes in navy, white, and gray; her long list of foods she couldn't eat and the longer list of foods she refused to even try, the inflexible daily schedule into which Michael had been fit. But there was something real and earthy about a woman who would ride the length of the country alone, and something very attractive about the way she flexed when her plans fell apart. He really admired that and, as ridiculous as it sounded even to him, he wanted to spend a little more time with her.

He was still wrestling these thoughts in his head when he strode into Nicki's kitchen and presented the eggs with a loud "Ta-da!" But he sensed immediately that something was wrong. A small group was clustered around Nicki's kitchen table and no one seemed to be hurrying to make breakfast.

"Good morning?" he called, more of a question than an assertion.

Nicki looked up from the table. Jennie too. They were talking to his old friend, Pete, otherwise known as PC Campbell, or PC Pete, as Michael liked to call him. PC Pete had a reputation for planning his beat around certain villagers' tea and coffee times, but this didn't look like a friendly chit-chat. A fourth person was at the table too. It took him a moment to piece together the voice and the brief glimpse of the person he'd seen before he realized who it was: Sarah.

His heart did a quick backflip when he realized she

hadn't left without saying goodbye after all. He caught himself beaming, until Nicki shot him a hard stare and he realized he had walked into the middle of a serious discussion.

"Everything okay?" he said. Why did people always ask that when it was abundantly clear that everything was far from okay?

"We've got a bit of a problem," said Nicki.

"My bike's been stolen," said Sarah, her voice wavering. Her face was red and her expression so fierce that Michael felt the urge to take a step backward.

"Right from the shed, right from under our noses," added Jennie, for dramatic effect.

"I was all packed, ready to leave, and when I went to the shed, she was gone," Sarah said, her voice rising with every word. "I can't believe somebody took Cecelia."

"Cecelia?" Michael asked, confused, but no one elaborated.

"Unfortunately," said Pete, as gently as he could, "we see this sort of theft more often than we'd like. Odds are it was someone from outside the village, probably part of an organized ring, which means it could be anywhere by now."

"But someone must have seen something," said Sarah. "I mean it was right behind a house with a dozen people inside. Surely someone in the village would have seen something unusual."

"We'll certainly make enquiries, Miss," said Pete. "But if I were you, I'd make alternative transportation plans."

"Alternative plans? You don't understand. This wasn't just a bike, it was..." She shook her head. Whatever she was going to say, she changed her mind. "Cecelia was... the bike was... special to me, that's all. If there's any chance of finding her, it would mean a lot to me."

Michael's guess was that the bike was an expensive gift from the fiancé, in which case the thieves were most likely rubbing their hands with glee right about now.

"Listen," he said, directing his words to the group, but looking at Sarah. "Someone might have seen something but not realized it was significant. So, let's use the calling tree."

"The what?" Sarah asked.

"Just come with me to the house," he said. "Oh, and bring your phone."

In his kitchen, Michael pulled out a card and placed it on the old oak table for Sarah to see. "I got the idea from my corporate life," he told her, pointing to the web of lines, names, and phone numbers. "It was a contingency plan we had in place in case anything catastrophic happened. A lot of companies implemented it after September 11. We had this tree set up, a bit like a family tree, so that everybody in the company was responsible for reaching three other people. That way we could check on everyone really quickly."

"You couldn't just send a group email?"

"Like I say, it was an emergency resource in case the power went out or there was a disaster or some other catastrophic failure of the communication network. We never had to use it, fortunately, but not long after I moved back here, Maddy disappeared."

"Maddy?"

"My niece. My sister Kate's daughter. A couple of years ago she went missing and no one knew where she was. Kate was beside herself, obviously, and so she stayed at home with George, my nephew, while Nicki and I went out to look for Maddy. We told every person we met and asked them to tell three other people. People called their friends and relatives in surrounding areas and by the end of the day we had hundreds of people looking for her."

"Did you find her?" Sarah asked her face crumpled with worry.

"The farmer over at High Top found her under a sheep bridge as he was heading in for the evening. She told him she was playing hide-and-seek, but of course he knew she wasn't, so he brought her home. But if he hadn't known she was missing she might have been out alone all night." Michael had told this story countless times, but whenever he got to this part he always went weak. He hated to think about how the story might have ended if Maddy hadn't been found. The possibilities were endless and almost none of them good. "After that I set up this calling tree as a way to rally everyone on short notice. So far we've used it three times, all of them to find Old Mrs. Whitaker. But since she went to live with her daughter, we haven't needed it."

"Do you think it might find my bike?" Sarah asked.

Michael smiled at her and a warm feeling blossomed in his belly. What he was doing was hardly heroic, by any standards, but it gave him a certain feeling of pride when he could use his tree to help, and he felt an extra good feeling that he could use it to help Sarah.

"Let's find out," he said. He shook off all the visions in his head of rescuing a damsel in distress. Sarah didn't need rescuing, she just needed some help and he was the man for the job.

Within half an hour, they had three reports of an unmarked white van in the area and two other people who'd seen two men and a woman walking slowly through a neighboring village in the early hours of the morning. Why no one had thought to report these activities at the time, Michael couldn't say. What was important was that they had the information now. It might be too late, as PC Pete said, to retrieve Sarah's bike, but at least he felt as if he'd done something productive.

"I'm sorry I wigged out earlier," Sarah said. "It's just a bike and I have insurance, but…"

Michael waited for her to explain why it was more than "just a bike" but she said nothing. Probably embarrassed to mention this fiancé, if he was guessing.

"Anyway, thank you for all your help," she said. "It means a lot."

"It's me who should be thanking you. My ladies laid a dozen eggs this morning."

Sarah's face lit up. "Really? The singing worked?"

Michael grinned. "Seems you're something of a chicken whisperer."

"Maybe I can try it again."

"I thought you were leaving today."

Sarah shrugged. "Well, I'm not going anywhere without a bike."

"Could you borrow one? Maybe someone in the village would lend you one."

"Thanks," she said, "but I'm not sure my bottom would appreciate riding a couple of hundred miles in someone else's saddle. Plus, I feel as if I should stick around for a day or two in case my bike turns up."

Michael was still thinking about Sarah's bottom perched on a narrow saddle and it took him a moment to realize what else she'd said. "Stay here?" he said at last, sounding like a dope.

"There are worse places," she said, and gave him a warm smile.

It was that smile that buoyed his fortitude and prompted him to ask. "Well, if you're staying," he said, "you really shouldn't miss the Midsummer Festival on Friday."

Sarah looked curious.

"It's sort of the big deal around here. It's always a good time."

Sarah seemed to consider this for a moment. "Sounds great. If my bike hasn't turned up by then, maybe I'll stay for the fair. In the meantime, I want to thank you for your help." She looked around the kitchen. "Is there anything I can do?"

"You can absolutely sing to my chickens again, and if you've nothing else to do, I can always use an extra set of hands in the garden."

She smiled and pushed up from the table. "I need to check with Nicki that she has a vacancy for me, and I have to file an official report on Cecelia, but tomorrow I'm all yours."

Before she'd even reached his garden gate, he was on the phone to his sister. "I don't care if you have to move another guest out to my barn, you have to make her room available."

"Michael," Nicki said. "Are you about to make a fool of yourself?"

"Probably," Michael said. "But what else would be new?"

____

CHAPTER SIX

THAT EVENING, Sarah pressed the phone to her ear and listened to the chirping ringtones. She couldn't decide if she wanted Amir to answer or if it would be easier if the call went straight to voicemail and she could say what she needed to say without him wigging out.

He picked up on the third ring.

"Where on Earth are you?" he asked. "I've been worried half to death."

But not so worried that you thought to ring. "I'm staying at a little B&B. I'm fine."

"Good lord. Why the devil didn't you let Guillaume take you to one of the other properties? Who knows if these little family-run places are clean?"

Sarah looked around the spotless room. She'd seen Nicki brandish a feather duster. No self-respecting speck of dirt would dare settle itself in her line of fire. "The place is nice," she said, deciding not to add, "You'd like it."

"I'm sure it's very quaint. I imagine the bed bugs are quite friendly, too. Enjoy your camping and I'll have Guillaume make a reservation at Dale Brook. You should be passing there on Friday, so I'll get you booked for two nights."

She pictured Amir looking at the route map she'd created. She'd spent hours planning this trip, looking at maps, evaluating road conditions and elevation gains, poring over cycling websites to calculate the ideal mix of riding and rest. Amir had finally given up trying to talk her out of the trip and instead insisted she leave a copy of every single detail for him. If anything happened to her, he'd know exactly where she was supposed to be. It was meant to be comforting, but a part of her had wished she could divert from the planned route, just for the freedom of knowing no one, not even Amir, would know where she was. Well, she'd got what she'd wished for, and now she was going to have to tell Amir about her change of plans.

"Actually," she said, "I'm going to stay here another night, maybe two. I'm more tired than I thought, and I need to work on the bike."

"What's wrong with the bike?"

"Nothing," she said, way too quickly. "It just needs an adjustment or two, and so do I."

There was a long pause on the other end of the phone.

"You're not worried, are you?" she asked.

"Of course I am. I'm always worried about you. It's just... I'd hoped you'd be home sooner, that's all. I miss you. And Mother wants us to firm up the new wedding plans so she can start making calls."

Sarah held in a sigh. *Mother. Of course.* It was always Mother holding the reigns.

When Sarah had first met Amir's family, she had been envious of how close they were. She loved their weekend jaunts to Amir's family home and was swept up in the constant stream of relatives who came to visit. His mother, Claudette, had been cool at first, prying information out of Sarah about her background. Sarah had bent the truth a little and left out the details of the red reminder bills and her mother's string of gentleman friends. Sarah knew Claudette would have preferred her son to bring home a wealthy heiress or even foreign royalty, anyone other than a grant writer for a wildlife rescue charity, whose bloodline included a drunkard, an ex-con, and a woman with the worst taste in men. But when it became clear that Amir was serious and determined to marry Sarah, Claudette had resigned herself. She accepted Sarah as part of the family… until Sarah and Amir had announced they were calling the wedding off.

It had been Sarah's doing, of course, but Amir had covered for her and told his mother it was a mutual decision. She owed him for that. But the wedding… the wedding had, well… the wedding had got away from her, completely out of control.

She'd wanted a country wedding, and Amir had agreed, but their idea of a "country wedding" had varied greatly. In fact, his idea of a country wedding had in no way resembled hers, other than in the end result, that she would become his wife. And once Claudette got involved, the whole thing had become more of a circus than a wedding. When Sarah realized she could fund the wildlife sanctuary for a year with the money they would spend on the wedding, she'd tried to wrestle back control, to tone things down and get her plans back on track. But it was like a runaway train and the only option left for Sarah to regain control and get the real wedding of her dreams was to let the train jump the tracks.

A month before the wedding, she'd called the whole thing off. She cancelled the London caterers, the same ones that did the BAFTAs, the florist who'd turned down the wedding of a minor royal for them, and the booking at Hillingham House. She'd notified her six bridesmaids and four flower girls, the page boys, groomsmen, and the string quartet. She'd canceled the jazz ensemble and the DJ, and the four-tier cake. And then she'd sat down with a bottle of wine and an entire vegetarian pizza and hand-addressed envelopes to send notices of the postponement to the three-hundred-and-twenty-four invited guests.

And there, right there, was the key to where it had all gone wrong. Of those three-hundred-and-twenty-four guests, Sarah had met fewer than a third, had personally invited twenty, and was related to exactly three: her mother, brother, and a cousin she hadn't seen in years. Amir's statistics had been more impressive, with a big contingent of acquaintances and a vast network of relatives. The rest of the guests, in fact the majority of the guests, had been business associates, friends, and acquaintances of Claudette. Sarah had written notes to at least one sheik to let him know that he could cancel his private jet for the weekend of June 15, because the wedding he was planning to attend was no more.

Claudette had turned into an iceberg worthy of sinking the Titanic, but Sarah had stood her ground, and Amir had stood beside her. It wasn't the marriage that had given Sarah cold feet, not at all; it was the wedding. And so, she had called it off.

And now she was lying to her fiancé.

"Tell her not to worry," Sarah said. "I just need the time you promised me and then I'll come home."

"I know," he said. "I trust you."

Sarah's throat tightened to keep down the lie she had told. Because if she told Amir that she was no longer in possession of her bike, he'd make calls and pull favors, or, more likely, swoop in to rescue her. And as much as she wanted her bike back, this was a battle she wanted to fight for herself, if only to prove that she could stand on her own two feet.

If she was going to stay, she might as well make herself useful. There was nothing she could do but wait to see if the calling tree turned up Cecelia. In the meantime, she didn't want to sit around thinking about Amir or his mother or the new set of wedding plans she was supposed to be forming. She had offered to pay back Michael for his kindness, so she'd better get to work.

After breakfast the next morning, she laid out all the clothes she'd brought with her. Packing for the ride had been a challenge. She couldn't just throw everything she owned into a giant suitcase and tow it behind her. Every piece of clothing had been carefully considered for weight, durability, washability, and versatility. Was it lightweight so as not to make her bike heavy? Would it stand up to be worn almost daily for two weeks? Could she wash it in a guest room sink and would it dry overnight hung on a shower rail? And finally, did it go with at least two other components of her wardrobe? In the end she'd opted for a pair of light-weight trousers and a knee-length skirt, three coordinated t-shirts, one with long sleeves, and a lightweight hoodie that went with them all, plus one cotton dress in case she ventured out of her room at Atherton Hall. So far, except for the dress, they had all proven to be excellent choices. But now she had nothing to wear, well, nothing that she was willing to get dirty. But she couldn't go out in her undies, so she opted for the trousers and her darkest t-shirt.

Downstairs, Nicki gave her the once over and shook her head. "Are you going to work in the muck or are you going out for shopping and a ladies' lunch?"

"It's all I've got."

Nicki rolled her eyes and disappeared into the living quarters, telling Sarah to wait. A moment later she came back and handed Sarah a pile of folded clothes. "Not quite as stylish, I'll admit, but much better suited to the task at hand, I think."

"Are you sure?" Sarah asked.

Nicki gave her a quick smile and indicated for her to go back up to her room. Sarah took this as a yes. "Thanks," she said.

Sarah slipped out of her own clothes and shook out the ones Nicki had lent her. They had a slightly musty smell, as if they'd been stashed in a drawer for some time, but there was the vague hint of faded lavender, the real stuff, dried in little hand-sewn sachets and tied with yarn, like her grandmother used to make. It made Sarah nostalgic for the woman who'd been the one stable part of her childhood.

Sarah had spent most summers with her brother, Luke, at Grandma Lily's. When she was a young girl, they'd traveled by train, out of whatever gray, damp city they happened to be living in at the time, and down to Cornwall. Somewhere on the way to the southwest peninsula of the country, the landscape changed, the clouds seemed to lift and the sun shone on the green, rugged countryside. Sarah knew that hadn't actually happened, as she could recall many a summer spent with her nose pressed against Grandma Lily's kitchen window, watching the rain pelt sideways across the sea. But at the time the trip had been enchanting. She had many fond memories of exploring the coves and beaches with Luke, collecting shells or yellow and black cinnabar moth caterpillars. They'd pretended they were pirates, reenacting the tales of smugglers and rum runners that Grandma loved to tell. She could still feel the scratch of long dune grass against her bare legs and the taste of fresh fish brought in straight from the harbor. And of course, Grandma Lily's homemade scones smeared with her own jam and globs of rich clotted cream. They were good memories of a simpler time in her life.

When their father left and their mother couldn't cope, they stayed the entire summer with Grandma Lily. Luke had refused to talk about his dad, but Grandma Lily had held them both close, assured them she would always be there for them, and when Sarah was ready to talk, Grandma Lily had been willing to listen. She wished she could sit down with her now and tell her about Amir and the wedding and this strange feeling of uncertainty that was creeping in to the pit of her stomach. But Grandma Lily hadn't kept her promise to be there forever. It had been three years since she'd passed away and Sarah missed her every day.

Sarah shook off the melancholy that had settled over her and climbed into Nicki's clothes. She pulled on the moss green trousers and pink t-shirt, and fastened the bottom two buttons of the purple and blue checked overshirt. She glanced at herself in the mirror and caught a glimpse of the little girl she'd once been. Not one item of clothing matched with another. Still it would be rude to complain and Nicki had been more than generous, after all. But honestly, she hoped she wouldn't run into anyone she knew. And she hoped that Michael wouldn't care.

At the back door Nicki handed her a pair of red and

black polka dot wellies. Sarah blanched. She'd once owned a pair just like them.

"Don't tell me. They don't match your outfit," Nicki said, assessing Sarah.

"Well," Sarah began.

"Ah, live a little," Nicki said. "It will do you good to shake things up a bit. You can't go through your whole life being perfectly coordinated. Sometimes it does a person good to look like they fell off the jumble sale table."

Sarah forced a smile. She wasn't about to tell Nicki that she'd spent most of her childhood in second-hand clothes. She stuffed her feet into the wellies and set off through the village.

She passed several familiar faces on the way to Michael's place. Everyone greeted her with a friendly smile and "G'mornin'" and "Lovely day." Not one person dropped their eyes to her "eclectic" outfit. In London, people might have crossed the street to avoid her if she'd gone out dressed like this. Here, either no one noticed or they didn't care. Sarah found it very refreshing.

She found Michael on his hands and knees, his head hidden by a hedge of climbing runner beans. His jeans were worn at the seat and a rip in the back exposed a sliver of thigh. He had strong legs, not bulky like cyclist's legs, but lean and toned and long and...

"Morning," said a voice, lifting Sarah from what, she had to admit, had been an overly long, but quite delicious daydream. Somewhere in her dreaminess, Michael had rocked back on his heels and was peering at her from underneath the brim of a straw fedora. His dark curls flipped up around the edges in a way that made Sarah want to reach out and tuck them in.

"Oh." She startled. "Hi. Um. I just... I actually. I'm here to help."

He stood up and dusted dried dirt from his knee. And smiled. He had a crooked smile that caused a curved crease between one cheek and his close-trimmed beard. When he smiled like that, his pale blue eyes lit like little chips of ice catching the polar sun.

"Also, I wanted to apologize."

"For what?"

Sarah sighed. "I overreacted about the bike yesterday. I was rude. I'm sorry."

"You already apologized. Sounds like it was a nice piece of machinery. Can't blame you for being upset. But I'm guessing it was more than the money. A gift?"

"I bought it myself, actually." She hesitated. It had been so much more than just a bike. Cecelia had been the first valuable item she'd ever bought for herself. She'd added custom components as she could afford them, until she'd built herself the bike of her dreams. It wasn't just a valuable piece of machinery. Cecelia was one of a kind. And the rusted bell with the cartoon lamb picture had been one of the few possessions she'd carried from childhood.

But even that didn't explain the feeling she had for the bike. She'd been thinking about it while she lied to Amir about her reason for staying. It wasn't the bike itself she was mourning, even though she had loved it. It was what it represented to her: Freedom. When she rode Cecelia through the streets of London, along the side of the Thames, or out into the hills of Surrey, she could truly be alone with her thoughts. Cecelia reminded Sarah that she could make it on her own, if she chose to. The bike was her own personal symbol of freedom and self-reliance.

As a child, she'd owned a bike for exactly three months. Their mother had moved her and Luke to an end terrace flat in the dingiest corner of a Midlands city. The neighbor downstairs had a son who'd outgrown his bike and come by a new one under dubious circumstances. But the neighbor had given the old bike to Sarah. That bike had given her her first taste of freedom. She'd been able to ride to a nearby park, see real trees, stop and sit on the grass, even hear birds. Grandma Lily had given her the bell with the lamb on it, and Sarah had loved the cheery sound it made as she zipped around the narrow streets.

But when they'd moved three months later, her mother had made her give the bike back. The neighbor had said she could keep it but their mother had insisted they weren't a charity case. She told Sarah she could have another bike after they moved, and so Sarah had taken the bell with her. She never did get the promised bike but she thought about it for almost fifteen more years and, as soon as she could afford it, she'd bought herself a used Trek bike and fastened on Grandma Lily's lamb bell. She was twenty-five years old before she'd been able to save enough money for the upgraded Specialized frame and hydraulic disk brakes, and she'd been adding custom components ever since. But she'd always kept the bell. The fact that someone had stolen that from her was a personal violation. Not just the loss of property but the taking away of everything Sarah held dear: security, pride, and most of all, freedom. She could afford to replace the bike and probably the upgrades, but she could never replace the meaning... or the little bell.

Only when she noticed Michael gaping at her did she realize how much of that she'd said out loud.

She looked away, embarrassed at telling a stranger the deepest parts of her soul. Now he'd think she was truly weird. "Anyway, I wanted to thank you for your help with the calling tree. So put me to work before I tell all my darkest secrets."

She didn't think doing a few garden tasks was too generous an offer, considering the help he'd given, but the way Michael's face lit up, you'd have thought she'd offered him a million pounds. Now who was the weird one?

CHAPTER SEVEN

"RIGHT," said Sarah as she strode up Michael's garden path. "Put me to work."

"Do you feel like planting? Harvesting? Mucking out?"

"Whatever will be most helpful," she said, quietly hoping he wouldn't say mucking out. She liked the chickens well enough, but they didn't half stink.

"Well, you can sow some more peas if you like."

"Just show me what to do."

Michael looked her up and down and she was sure he was going to question her abilities, but instead, he grabbed a rake and some packets of seeds and indicated for her to follow.

"We'll plant them in rows, here," he said, pointing to an empty strip of ground. "It's been tilled so you just need to go down the row and loosen the soil with a rake, knock out any big lumps." He leaned into the rake and moved it back and forth across the soil. The muscles in his arms flexed and stretched as he moved, working hard. She and Amir were members of a gym in London, where most of the members stood preening in front of the wall of mirrors while they moved weights up and down in a linear motion. Amir's personal trainer had shown him exercises to isolate individual muscle groups, to break down the fibers and build them up. Amir was tall and lean, his olive skin stretched over well-defined muscles. "Cut" is how he'd say it. But Michael's arms weren't like that. His forearms were sinewy and his shoulders broad, but she could see from the way he moved that his whole body was strong, working in the way it was designed, the muscles all pulling together. Amir walked like he had a coat hanger still stuck in his jacket. Michael's movements were fluid.

"Like this," he was saying as Sarah realized she hadn't been paying attention. "If you can sow then evenly and finely, it means I won't have to thin them later."

"My grandma had a little vegetable patch in her garden. She hated thinning seedlings. She always said it was a shame to waste them."

"She's right. And when you manage a big plot like this alone, anything you do to make things more efficient means more time for other jobs."

"What on earth made you decide to do this alone?" she asked.

He gave her a sheepish look and Sarah had the feeling she'd waded into dangerous territory. "I didn't do it alone, at least not at first. I was living in London, totally miserable. I was stressed out and overworked, indoors all the time. I had a good job and a nice life, but something was missing and I didn't know what. Then my folks decided they couldn't keep the place up anymore. They wanted to buy a place in Spain and move to the warm weather. The three of us grew up here—me, Nicki, and Kate—and it just seemed like the right time to make a big change. I talked my fiancée-at-the-time into moving here with me. It was a big adventure at first. Country living, the simple life." He poked at a clod of dirt with the rake. Sarah waited in silence, not wanting to push him if he didn't want to talk about it. "Anyway," he said at last, "one weekend we were invited to visit some old friends in London, get away for a couple of days. One of the chickens wasn't well, so I decided to stay."

"And she went without you?"

"And didn't come back." He turned up his mouth in a sort of smile, but his lips were pressed together so hard they turned almost white.

"So you were stuck here alone."

"I always had this idea that doing something hard with the right person at your side makes it an adventure."

"And she didn't agree."

"Or she just wasn't the right person," he said. "She's marrying my friend, or former friend, so I suppose it wasn't meant to be."

Sarah nodded but couldn't think of the right thing to say. When Claudette began horning in on the wedding plans, Sarah kept telling herself that it was worth giving in to Claudette if it meant having Amir. Amir kept telling her not to worry, that the secret with Claudette was to let her feel like she was running the show, but to do your own thing anyway. The only trouble was, they hadn't done it their way. At every turn, Amir had said, "just let her have it her way; it'll make for a quiet life." And so they'd ended up with Claudette's vision of the wedding, and Sarah had finally pulled the plug. But in the week that Sarah had spent riding Cecelia through the countryside, she'd had time to think, not just about the wedding but about her life with Amir.

When she'd first met Amir at a fundraiser to buy new incubators for the sanctuary, the attraction had been physical. Even in a room full of sharp-dressed men, Amir had stood out as exceptionally handsome. When she realized who he was, she'd made a point of talking to him in the hopes of cajoling a donation from him. But Amir had surprised her. He'd talked passionately about his love of the countryside, the importance of protecting all endangered creatures, not just the big impressive ones. He'd told her funny stories about his boyhood antics on his grandmother's country estate, and his time as a student at Cambridge. And when he invited her to join him on a weekend picnic, Sarah had agreed. He'd shown up in jeans and a button-down Oxford, looking even more handsome than in a tux, and produced a Harrods hamper packed with goodies. They talked all afternoon—or rather Amir had, telling how he'd spent a year in Paris, training in the finest hotels, and of learning the art of service on a diamond tycoon's luxury yacht in the Med. She in turn told him about Cecelia and their trip down the Danube and the tour of the Ring of Kerry when they hadn't seen a drop of rain.

It wasn't until after their third date—dinner at an unassuming London restaurant—that a check arrived at the sanctuary. Amir's donation had almost doubled their efforts from the fundraiser.

"I wanted to make sure you weren't just dating me for my money," he said, a mischievous twinkle in his eye.

"Incubators are a girl's best friend," Sarah said, and Amir had laughed.

But sometime between those carefree early days and the outrageous wedding, something had changed. Only now she had some distance from it did she see how often Amir cleaved to his mother's wishes for the sake of a quiet life.

"It will be different once we're married," he told her. "It will be just the two of us."

But Sarah wasn't so sure. Claudette had already hinted

that Sarah should leave the sanctuary and work in the family business. She made assumptions that their children would have nannies and go to the best schools. And now that Sarah saw how the wedding plans had gone, she wondered about his resolve to build a life of their own. Only now did she see that when things started getting hard, he hadn't been at her side. Or rather, he'd been at her side, but had one foot over the line on his mother's side.

"What about you?" Michael asked, handing her the seed packet and indicating that she should start sowing seeds. "What would prompt a perfectly rational, sensible woman, which I'm assuming you are, to ride a bike four hundred miles in an unpredictable climate like ours?"

Sarah focused on the seed packet, not really wanting to tell Michael the sordid details of her cancelled wedding, the niggling feeling that she was signing up for Claudette's life. Claudette had blown up and lost her cool, and it was Amir who'd suggested Sarah get away for a while to give him the chance to placate his mother. "It was something I always wanted to do and then this summer I found myself at a loose end for a couple of weeks and decided it was now or never."

"It's quite the undertaking. So, what do you do, just ride as far as you can each day and find a place to stay when you get tired?"

Sarah laughed. "No. I planned the whole route ahead and booked in advance. I like to know where I'm going to put my head down every night."

"That doesn't leave much room for adventure."

That word again. Adventure. The truth was, the old Sarah would have done exactly that, set off and gone where her wheels took her. But Amir had been worried and so, to put his mind at ease, she'd planned the route and left him with a detailed itinerary.

"What if you have unanticipated interruptions. What if you get a flat tire or you get lost?" Michael asked.

"I don't get lost," she said, defensively.

"What if you pass somewhere so beautiful and fascinating—like here for example—that you have to stop and look around?"

"I can always come back."

Michael gave her a skeptical look. "So no flexibility, no spontaneity, no spur of the moment?"

"Well, not until my bike was stolen."

"Fair point," he said. "And what does your fiancé think about this?"

Sarah's head shot up. "My fiancé?"

"Forgive me but I couldn't help noticing the rock on your finger. I'm very sharp, a bit of a Sherlock Holmes, and I deduced that there might be a fiancé involved."

Sarah's face burned. "Brilliant deduction," she said. "Amir. My fiancé." The word stuck to the dry roof of Sarah's mouth.

"Are you sure?" Michael said.

"Sure of what?"

"That he's your fiancé. You sound a bit uncertain."

Sarah sighed. "Well, if someone is still technically a fiancé after you've called off the wedding, then yes."

"Oh," said Michael. "I'm sorry. I didn't mean to pry."

Sarah waved him off. "Nothing to be sorry about. The plan to get married is still in place, just the plan for that particular wedding is on hold."

Michael looked confused. Sarah couldn't blame him. By this time she was more than used to people's confusion as she tried to explain how the perfect wedding hadn't been so perfect after all. She was fully aware that it made her sound spoiled and difficult when she explained that the wedding hadn't been what she wanted. Even more so when she'd explained it was too ostentatious.

"Have you ever felt as if you were living someone else's life?" she asked.

"What do you mean?"

"Like you've been living your life, fully in control, making decisions and pointing yourself in a certain direction and it's all going to plan. And then one day you look up and realize you've had it all wrong. You haven't been creating the life you really want; you've been creating the life you thought you wanted, but really that life was made for someone else. And you realize you're not even the person you thought you were, so how can you possibly know what you want? And so you call the whole thing off and run away to somewhere safe until the dust settles."

Sarah swallowed, wishing she could pull all those words back inside. All she had to say was that the wedding had grown out of control, but instead she'd blurted every hysterical detail, including some bits she'd never even admitted to herself. Because it wasn't just the wedding, was it? It was Claudette and her control, not just of the wedding but of Amir. And the further Sarah had pedaled from London, the more her doubts about her life with Amir had grown. But she didn't need to tell Michael all that. He was going to think she was a complete nut job.

But Michael just stared at her like he was looking into the depths of her soul. "How do you think I ended up here, living alone except for a clutch of temperamental chickens?"

"Adventure?"

Michael laughed. "Something like that."

He smiled but turned away so she couldn't read his face. There was more to his story than he was letting on. Sarah picked up the rake and set about breaking up the rough ground, chipping away at the lumps of dirt until they gave way and broke apart. She poked and chopped until the dirt was smooth, a safe place for the little pea seeds to take root and grow.

CHAPTER EIGHT

SARAH DUSTED the dirt from her trousers and stretched her aching back. She thought she was in pretty good shape, flexible from her yoga classes and strong from her gym workouts and cycling, but this was hard physical work and she would be sore the next day. Not ideal for the riding she'd have to do to stay on schedule, she thought, then remembered that she wouldn't be riding because she no longer had a bike. What she wanted more than anything was to go to her room, soak in the bath, and take the longest nap in the history of long naps. But she was pretty sure planting a couple of rows of peas wasn't an equal trade for Michael's efforts in searching for Cecelia, and she didn't want him to think she was either feeble or ungrateful.

"Fancy a cuppa?" She turned to find Michael, wiping his face with a polka dot bandana.

"I could kill for one," she said, thinking that she couldn't care less about the tea, but if it meant sitting down for even five minutes she'd take it.

"The tea shack," he said, pointing to a wooden structure at the bottom of the garden.

She followed him down the path, butterflies flitting in front of her as she went. The air hummed with the sound of insects and the warm breeze ruffled the tassels of corn and flapped the leaves of bean plants like bunting. It would have all been entirely heavenly had Sarah's legs and back not been screaming.

Michael pulled open the door of a run-down shed. The rusted hinges creaked and a few flecks of peeling paint drifted off in the breeze, but inside was the tiniest, coziest-looking living room. There was a worn rug on the floor and two threadbare armchairs arranged around an electric heater. On an upturned milk crate was a hot plate, a kettle, and a set of mismatched mugs.

"Make yourself at home," Michael said and Sarah flopped into the nearest chair. She sank so deeply into the cushion that it seemed to wrap around her. She closed her eyes and in seconds was asleep.

She dreamed she was riding her bike up a long steep hill that never seemed to end. Just when she thought she was nearing the top, Claudette stepped out and directed her around a bend where the hill continued up. All the while she pedaled, someone was singing a sweet little song.

Sarah's eyes flitted open and she blinked to get her bearings. Michael sat opposite her, his chin dropped to his chest. At first she thought he had fallen asleep too, but she could still hear the song that was in her dream, as if Michael had been singing. She blinked herself awake. It *was* Michael singing. His arms were folded to his chest and cupped in his hands sat Zorro. The top buttons of Michael's shirt were open and he pressed the little chick to his chest, crooning a song as he stroked the chick's head. Sarah held her breath, not wanting to make a sound and disturb them. She watched as Michael petted the little chick. He was so gentle with it, soothing it with a quiet hum and tender strokes. Zorro huddled against Michael's chest, her round black eyes flitting closed and open, closed and open, until she finally fell asleep. Sarah's own eyes flitted closed again. She imagined her head against Michael's chest, the feel of his fingers as he gently stroked her hair. She drifted off to sleep again, the hum of his song and the beating of his heart beneath her ear.

Her eyes flew open and she blinked herself wide awake. She looked at her Apple Watch. It was almost noon. How long had she been asleep? How long had she been sitting there imagining her head on Michael's chest?

"I should go," she said, sitting up and making Michael start, which in turn woke Zorro.

"Your tea's gone cold," he said. He had such a warm, gentle smile, the kind that you could trust. But how much could you trust a man who sang lullabies and lured you to sleep in his shed? "I was about to go in to make some lunch. Can I offer you a sandwich?"

Sarah shook her head, trying to stop the words "yes, please" from making it to her lips. "I should go," she said.

Michael looked disappointed, but when she stood to leave, he got up too. "Thanks for all your help today."

"It was nothing."

"It was everything."

She looked away, embarrassed.

"I usually go down to The Butcher's Arms on a Thursday evening, meet up with some friends. Why don't you come down and have a drink?"

Sarah hesitated. "I don't know."

"It's quiz night."

"I'll think about it," she said, inching for the door. "Thanks for the offer anyway."

She gave him a quick wave and hurried out of the shed. She didn't slow down until she was back in her room at Sunnydale.

Sarah ran hot water into the big claw-foot tub and stepped out of her dirty clothes. Her body ached but her skin felt alive with the fresh air and the satisfaction of hard work outdoors. She pushed open the bathroom window so the breeze blew in and caressed her skin. It made her feel free and at one with nature. Made her want to roll naked in the grass... which obviously she would never do. She pulled the diamond engagement ring from her finger and examined the stone. She should have taken it off before she stuck her hands in the dirt, but she hadn't taken it off since the day Amir had given it to her. She was surprised by how easily it slid over her knuckle. She hadn't been carrying much in the way of excess weight at the beginning of her trip, but a week of pedaling day after day had burned through a lot of calories, despite the efforts of every B&B owner, pub landlord, and restauranteur to fatten her up and put some meat on her bones. But now, the ring that had been so carefully and precisely created for her under Amir's direction slipped from her finger as if it had been made for someone else.

She looked at the perfect diamond he had selected: a princess cut of the best clarity that shone like a cube of glacial ice from her finger. He'd designed the ring around the stone, and presented it to her on one knee. Amir's taste was impeccable, and the ring was stunning. Literally stunning, and that was the problem. When Sarah had shown it to her colleagues at the rescue center, they had gaped with their mouths open, leaving Sarah feeling embarrassed. They'd recovered quickly, telling her how beautiful it was and marveling at the way it caught the sunlight, scattering perfect drops of light across any surface. But Sarah saw in their eyes what she already felt in her heart: Yes, the ring was gorgeous, but it was showy and audacious when simple and unassuming was much more her style.

Her mother's ring had been a simple gold band, with a tiny chip of a diamond in a modest setting. Once, when Sarah was young, her mother had taken off the ring and let Sarah try it on. Perched on the edge of her parents' bed, Sarah had proclaimed the ring the most beautiful thing she had ever seen and announced that she wanted one just like it when she got married.

"Well, I hope you get something a little bit fancier than that," her mum had said. "But it's not the ring that makes the marriage, my love. Remember that."

"I know," Sarah had said. "It's the boy. And I'm going to make sure I marry someone lovely. Like Daddy."

Her mother had taken back the ring and turned it in her palm. Sarah waited for her mother to say more, but finally she'd slipped the ring onto her finger and hurried Sarah downstairs for dinner.

Years later, after Sarah saw her parents' relationship in a new light, she wondered what her mother might have said that day. Did she know then that marrying someone like Daddy wasn't such a great idea? He'd been a good dad, at least as long as he'd been around, but he was a dreamer, always cooking up a new business idea, moving them to a new place for a fresh start, and always falling on his face. Her mother had compromised her whole life because of him. "Marriage is a give and take," had been another of her mother's sayings, but the giving had been largely one-sided. And when her father had been forced to choose between supporting his wife and children and chasing his dreams, he'd walked away and never looked back. "Money can't buy love"—another cliché her mother often trotted out. But when her parents' love had run out, there was no money left either. After that, Sarah had sworn to do better, to make compromises, of course, because that's what made relationships endure, but not to sacrifice everything for love. Why not have the boy *and* the ring?

It was possible to fall in love with a poor man, of course. In fact Sarah had done exactly that in college. She'd fallen hard for a political activist without two pennies to rub together. But it hadn't been poverty that had caused things to fall apart. Not at all. Philandering, drinking, and an unhealthy obsession with gambling had outweighed any lack of means. She'd fallen for someone just like Daddy after all.

So when she met Amir, she thought her mother would be thrilled. Love and a little security? Well, it was the perfect match. But when Sarah had announced their engagement and shown her the ring, her mother's reaction had surprised her. Rather than being elated, her mother had seemed sad. She liked Amir very much and told Sarah she'd be glad to have him as a son-in-law, but when she saw the ring, she fingered it thoughtfully, and gave Sarah a small hard-to-read smile.

"It's lovely," she said, when Sarah had finally prompted her for an opinion.

Sarah had nodded. "It is."

"But the ring doesn't make the marriage. You remember that, don't you?"

"I remember," Sarah said. "And I've got the boy, too."

And she did have the boy. She loved Amir and she wanted to get past the wedding and start her life with him. But as they'd made plans for the wedding and Claudette became involved, Sarah's mind flitted back to her mother's words. The ring didn't make the marriage, and nor did the wedding, and it wasn't long before she realized that Amir had grown detached. It was okay that he wasn't as involved in the wedding plans as she was; he was busy with the business, and he would be happy with whatever plans she made. But she soon realized she wasn't getting the small simple wedding she wanted; they were getting the wedding his mother wanted. And Sarah started to wonder if she was getting the man she wanted too. Because Amir was a man who let his mother take over. He would insist she didn't run his life, if pressed, but he had stepped into his role in the family business without question. He hadn't bothered with aspirations of becoming an astronaut or a fireman, like some little boys. He'd been expected to step in line with Claudette's plans for him to run the Hillingham Hotel Group, and he'd complied. Sometimes she wondered if she had been Amir's one act of rebellion, marrying a woman his mother didn't choose, but she pushed that thought aside. Amir loved her, of course he loved her.

But as their relationship unfolded and the wedding plans came together, Sarah realized that she might be marrying the man of her dreams, but he came as a package with his mother. The ring suddenly seemed like a consolation prize.

When the water in the tub had gone cold, Sarah climbed out and wrapped herself in a fluffy yellow towel. She stepped to the small bathroom window and let the fresh air caress her clean, damp body. From behind the curtain, she looked down at the early afternoon comings and goings of the villagers, until she found herself staring at the rows of beans and leafy squares of Michael's garden. What an interesting man he was, choosing this lifestyle when he could have had it easy. Maybe he'd been running away from his problems, too. Or maybe at some subconscious level he was running away from the wrong woman, knowing she wasn't cut out for this life. Poor guy. What kind of a woman would risk losing a man like that? Perhaps she would go to the pub tonight, get to know him better. Just for the sake of curiosity.

CHAPTER NINE

JAMIE WAS in his usual spot when Michael arrived at The Butcher's Arms. He looked like he was already three long sups down his pint but Michael was glad to see a second glass on the table waiting for him.

"Here he is, Casanova himself," said Jamie as Michael pushed his hair back from his face and perched on a low bar stool.

"What are you talking about?" Michael asked, although he already guessed that Jamie had heard something about Sarah. That was the one downside to living in a small village like Hope. Everyone knew everyone else's business.

"So who is she?" Jamie asked.

Michael made a confused face, like he had no clue what Jamie was talking about, but his cheeks burned hot. He and Jamie had been friends since their first day of primary school and sometimes knew one another better than they knew themselves. When Jamie had fallen in love with Harriet Belmont when they were sixteen, Michael had seen it coming long before Jamie had worked it out for himself.

The only thing Michael hadn't predicted was that "Harry" would break his friend's heart. As a former chef and owner of Local Goodness, a much sought-after local meal kit service, Jamie was the most eligible bachelor in the valley. His wild curls and impish smile only added to his charm. Trouble was, love never seemed to stick to him.

Of course, what did Michael know about sticky love? As his sister Kate once said, "The envelope that holds Caroline's heart is empty." Michael had said that was poetic but meaningless, but he understood it now. On paper Caroline had been perfect for him—both of them driven, focused, aiming to the top of their respective career ladders. And she had cared about him, still did, in her own way. But he wasn't sure now that she had ever really loved him. She certainly hadn't loved him enough to love only him. He'd convinced himself that Caroline wasn't really the marrying kind, but then she hadn't waited long to get herself attached again. So maybe he wasn't the marrying kind, not in the twenty-first-century way. His parents had been married for almost forty years, his grandparents more than sixty. And Michael had always wanted that kind of marriage, one person, through thick and thin, the good, the bad, and the ugly. He knew that kind of marriage took resilience and compromise. He knew it meant letting go of perfection, and he always thought it would be worth it, but he wasn't sure that was realistic these days.

Look at his friends, so many of them in and out of relationships, never settling down or never willing to settle. Even among his friends who had married, so few seemed to have an expectation of fidelity or longevity. It was more an attitude of "this is the one... for now." It was a product of the disposable society they lived in, where things weren't built to last. Everyone always had to have the best, newest, most fashionable. People camping out overnight to be the first to own a new kind of phone, even though the one they had worked perfectly well. Everything was built to be tossed these days, even marriages.

But his grandparents were always fixing things. His grandma darned socks and made old curtains into new cushion covers; his granddad refinished their ancient oak table (now Michael's) and kept an old van running for decades with used spare parts. Fixing things when they broke or lost their luster. Fixing, not discarding. But Caroline wasn't a fixer. She always wanted the new and shiny. And once she found it, he'd been tossed aside.

"Her name is Sarah," Michael said. "And she has a rock the size of a spaceship on her finger. I could buy chicken feed for a lifetime for what that thing is worth."

"I heard she ditched the wedding," said Jamie.

"But not the groom."

"And yet she's found a way under your skin."

Michael shook his head. "No way."

"Come on, mate. You've had a face like a wet Wednesday ever since you heard that Caroline is getting hitched. Then this Sarah turns up and you're happier than I've seen you in months."

"There's nothing there, believe me."

"And yet you asked her to come out for a drink tonight."

"Can't a man have any secrets around here?"

"And she must be interested if she said yes."

"She didn't say yes. Who told you she said yes?"

"Well, if she's the one with the big sexy eyes and the hair the color of wheat and a body that..."

"She's here, isn't she?"

"Straighten your hair, my friend; she's coming this way."

Michael stood up so fast, the stool toppled over and hit the ground.

"Cool move," said Jamie, which only made Michael's face burn hotter.

Jamie went to the bar to get Sarah a drink while Michael gathered his composure and pulled over a chair for her. She looked around the slightly tattered decor of the Butcher's Arms and Michael wished he'd suggested The White Swan instead. The Swan was what the locals called "the tourist pub." It served better food and was quieter, and Nicki always sent her guests there. But The Butcher's was for locals, a place to come and relax and catch up with friends. Not the place to try an impress someone like Sarah.

"I lived over a pub like this once," she said.

Michael raised his eyebrows.

"It was back when pubs still allowed smoking so our whole flat smelled like stale beer and cigarette smoke. Fortunately we didn't live there long enough to do any serious lung damage."

She laughed, but Michael sensed some melancholy in her tone. "Did you move a lot?"

Sarah laughed again. "All the time. By the time I was sixteen I'd lived in twelve different houses in seven different towns, and been to nine different schools." And she'd moved five more times since then.

Michael gaped. "I grew up in the house I live in now, lived in two places in London, and came back to where I started."

"That sounds like heaven."

"And he's had one friend his whole life," said Jamie, setting a pint of Guinness and a packet of salt and vinegar crisps in front of Sarah. "Me. Can't decide if he's the luckiest man alive or just a really sad git."

"Oh, lucky," Michael said, turning on his sarcasm. "Definitely lucky."

"So, what do you think of this self-sufficient thing?" Sarah asked.

Michael cringed, sure Jamie would make some smart-aleck comment to embarrass him.

"I thought he was mad, to be honest," Jamie said. "But it suits him. We could all stand to live a bit more simply. We'd be a lot happier."

Michael glanced at Sarah. She wasn't laughing. He wished he could see what she was thinking.

"I feel bad about her bike," Michael said after Sarah excused herself to go to the ladies' room. "Makes the village look bad."

"I doubt she'll see it again," Jamie said. "It'll be long gone now."

"I wondered about trying to replace it, to make up for it somehow."

"Sounds like you'd need a mortgage for that."

"Well, not replace it exactly. I have a frame in the barn that I could clean up and paint."

"I have a set of wheels from my old bike."

"I could use the calling tree and see if I could rustle up the rest of the parts. It wouldn't be anything like the one she lost, but it would show her not everyone around here is bad."

Jamie swilled what was left of his beer around in his glass.

"What?" Michael asked.

Jamie shook his head. "Nothing."

"You think it's the stupidest idea I've ever had."

"I don't actually," Jamie said.

"But?"

"But, if you try to tell me again you're not seriously in love with her, I'm going to flat out call you a liar."

"She's engaged," Michael said.

"Well, if she is," said Jamie, "how come she's not wearing that ring?"

CHAPTER TEN

AT THE GATE OF SUNNYDALE, Sarah wished Michael goodnight and let herself in at the front door, closing it quietly behind her. The village was already quiet and most of the B&B guests had already turned in for the night. There was a light on in the kitchen and the sound of music playing at a low volume. Sarah tiptoed over and peered through the gap in the door to the kitchen. Nicki was dancing to a disco tune Sarah recognized, wiggling her hips as she chopped a honeydew melon. The kitchen prep table was stacked with a giant sack of potatoes.

Suddenly, Sarah didn't feel tired. She wasn't ready to go up to bed alone. She wanted to be in company to soak up these new people for as long as she could.

"You can come in," Nicki said. She smiled but she didn't look up.

"Need some help?" Sarah asked, easing in to the kitchen.

"As a general rule, I prefer my guests not to prepare their own food," Nicki said. "It sort of goes against the whole point of running a bed and breakfast."

"I'm not sure I qualify as a typical guest anymore. Plus I like peeling potatoes. I find it relaxing. Not to mention I'm good at it." Sarah picked up a potato and turned it in her hand, taking off the skin with long, sweeping strokes, the way Grandma Lily had taught her.

"Don't let Jennie catch you then," Nicki said, "or she'll think you're after her job."

"Tell her not to worry; I'm staying for the fair and then I need to leave."

"Even if your bike doesn't turn up?"

Sarah shrugged. She couldn't imagine leaving without Cecelia, but she couldn't stay here forever. Even if she couldn't finish her ride, sooner or later she'd have to make her way home to Amir.

Nicki gave her a sideways glance. "Well, you'll be missed around here."

Sarah's face flushed hot, her thoughts pinging to Michael. "Really?"

"We get a lot of city people come up for the weekend. They fall in love with the place, daydream about how nice it would be to live here, but by the end of the weekend they're itching to get back. But not you. You fit right in."

"I could live here," Sarah said. She scraped at the potato, no longer able to keep up the long smooth passes. Only now that the words had tumbled out, did she think about what she'd said. She'd felt a sense of calm since she'd been here. She'd been stressed about the wedding, but the pace of the village had helped her to slow down and breathe. But it was more than that. She felt welcome here, comfortable in a way she seldom did anywhere else. The only other place she'd really ever felt that way was at Grandma Lily's. Even with Amir's family, she always felt like she had to be careful with her words. With Nicki, she felt like nothing was off-limits.

"What's the story with your brother?" she blurted, immediately wishing she'd at least tried to be a bit more subtle.

Nicki glanced at her and gave her an amused but knowing look. "You two seem awfully fascinated with one another all of a sudden."

"He's been asking about me?"

"More like talking non-stop."

"Oh," said Sarah. "Well, he's pretty interesting."

"Oh, yeah, he's fascinating," Nicki mumbled, barely looking up as she chopped the melon into neat cubes.

"I think he's really brave to do what he's done. I mean, how many people fantasize about throwing in their humdrum lives and living more simply?"

"Almost everyone who comes here, but it's a romantic idea, that's all. I honestly don't know many who dream of living like a hermit and shoveling chicken poo every day." Nicki stabbed at a cube of melon with a fork, skewering it with a little more force than Sarah felt was healthy. She popped it into her mouth.

"It sounds like you don't approve."

Nicki sighed and wiped her hands on a tea towel that hung from the belt of her apron. "It's noble," she said, "and I admire him taking a risk. And of course, I'm very happy to have him living close by again. Not to mention the added perk of the eggs and an extra pair of hands."

"But..." Sarah prompted.

"But..." Nicki shook her head and Sarah worried that she'd pushed too far and that Nicki would clam up on the topic of her brother. But she didn't. "But, I worry he's cutting himself off. Isolating himself."

Sarah couldn't see how Michael was doing that. The village was small, yes, but everyone was friendly. Michael seemed to know all his neighbors and she'd yet to meet anyone who didn't like him. On top of all that, both his sisters, whom he clearly adored, lived within walking distance from him. Sarah couldn't help but think that she'd do anything for that kind of life. It didn't seem isolated at all. "He's got you," she ventured. "And Kate. And he seems to love it here."

"Yeah," Nicki said. "You're right. I worry about him too much. It's the mothering instinct in me."

"Caroline really broke his heart, didn't she?"

"Ah, he's better off without her. I keep telling him that. I never liked her from the first time I met her, but Michael was besotted so I accepted her. She was always restless here, though. Course, I turned out to be right. That gave me no pleasure. But yes, she burned him. I suppose that's why I'm so protective of him. He's my little brother and I don't like it when someone tries to hurt him." She rolled a fresh melon onto the chopping board and sliced it in two with one firm blow, hitting the wood on the other side. Sarah wondered if it was Caroline's head Nicki pictured as she hacked. She hoped it wasn't hers.

Once in her room, Sarah's weary body sunk into the soft mattress and her cheeks burned from spending the day outdoors working. She felt as if she could drift into the deepest sleep of her life, and yet her mind was alive and busy as if it never wanted to sleep again. She couldn't help wondering if she'd been sleepwalking through her life. Sleepwalking through everyone else's dreams. She'd been present for all of it, watched it happening, and yet she'd been somehow disengaged, as if she'd dreamed the whole thing.

Take the wedding. She'd been explicit, stated her desire for a country wedding, simple, a gathering of friends and relatives—few that they were, in her case—to celebrate her marriage to the man she loved. In her vision of a country wedding, she'd pictured bridesmaids in flowered cotton dresses and pink wellies, the groom in tweed, a bouquet of flowers cut from the garden. She'd been wide awake and clear about what she wanted, so how had it got so out of hand? She'd just kept saying yes, that was the problem. She'd said yes to Amir, but really she'd been saying yes to Claudette. She'd had a vision of her dream wedding, but whenever Amir presented something new, she'd been distracted. The country house for the venue. Yes. The pavilion tent in the grounds. Well, of course that made sense, given the British climate. And the guest list growing from fifty close friends and family to a hundred. She'd still said yes and she'd kept saying yes as it ballooned to two hundred and three hundred, more than half of whom she wouldn't be able to pick out in a line-up if she ever saw them again. Business associates and clients of Claudette's, offspring of Amir's father's friends, relatives coming out of the woodwork like weeds springing up in an empty field. And yet Sarah had continued to say yes. Why had she continued to say yes when what she really wanted to say, to scream, was no, no, no, no, NO!

She knew the answer. Amir. She'd kept saying yes to Amir. Because everyone knew, everyone told her, how lucky she was to have snagged him. Even she knew how lucky she was. Amir took tall, dark, and handsome to a new level, with his chiseled good looks, his lean, slender body, and that caramel skin. He was Rudolph Valentino, dressed in Armani instead of robes, and traveling by Jaguar rather than horse. But it wasn't all superficial. Amir understood how important the sanctuary was to her and he'd used his assets to help her. He was kind and respectful, he anticipated her needs, not to mention her desires, and delivered on his promises. He always delivered on his promises. He was a fairytale, and Sarah, for all her common sense, had been captivated.

Captivated. Now there was a word. Captive, more like, because in the end Amir was a man used to getting his own way, accustomed to persuading people to his way of thinking, unused to being told no, and Sarah had been no more able to resist his charms than his business associates, his mother, or anyone else who met him. She'd postponed the wedding, not called it off. She hadn't said "no" to Amir; she'd only said, "Not yet." But now she wondered if that was really what she'd meant.

She rolled over and punched the screen of her phone, bringing it to life, and placed a call.

Amir answered on the fourth ring. He didn't sound like he'd been sleeping. "Just got back from dinner at Mother's. She asked about you. I was getting ready to send out a search party. Where are you?"

"Still here. I have something to tell you."

"I'm listening."

She told him about Cecelia and how the village had rallied to help find her. "But no luck."

"I have a late meeting tomorrow, but I'll come up this weekend."

"No." She calmed her voice. "I want to give it a couple more days to see if Cecelia turns up. Then I'll come home and we can talk about the wedding."

"Good," he said. "Because Mother is pestering me for a date."

Sarah pressed her lips together tight. He wanted to

know *when* they would get married, and her answer now might be "never."

CHAPTER ELEVEN

SARAH WAS ATTEMPTING to tame her hair that Friday evening when she heard a flurry of voices in the kitchen. Nicki was laughing, as usual, a teasing tone in her voice. Jennie chirped something, and then Sarah heard Michael's low voice, his gentle round laugh. It was such a soothing sound. There was nothing forced about it, nothing fake, he wasn't trying to impress anyone. She loved the easy way he laughed with his sister. She envied that kind of relationship.

She moved toward the open window and perched on the window ledge to listen. The sounds of the Midsummer Fair drifted in on the evening breeze as she strained to hear the conversation below. She couldn't make out any words, but she could sense the teasing tone, the love between the siblings. She could have been quite happy to sit there all night and just listen to that music, the sound of loving people enjoying one another's company. Amir had said he'd been to his mother's for dinner. She pictured him sitting at Claudette's immense dining room table with his family. She could imagine the rhythmic clink of silverware—real silverware—against bone china plates, the hushed tones of polite conversation, restrained laughter. She was glad she hadn't been there. She could only imagine the icicles Claudette would have flung across the polished oak at her, the criticisms and judgements, thinly veiled as astute observations and flippant comments, their frozen barbs slicing into Sarah's core.

A shriek rang out from the kitchen, followed by more laughter. What had Michael said this time to push Nicki's buttons? Sarah slid on her shoes and took a long look at herself in the mirror. Not too shabby.

Suddenly she felt nervous, like a teenager going on a date. But this wasn't a date... was it? Of course not. It was just an invitation to participate in the village fair. Warm, friendly people who wanted to make sure she had a memorable time while she was in their care.

So why did she suddenly feel uncomfortable?

She couldn't deny that she liked Michael. He was an attractive man. But he was a farmer, for pity's sake. A voluntary farmer, a man who'd chucked in a perfectly good life to subsist off the land. He was possibly deranged. Not to mention the very important point that she was engaged. To be married. To Amir. This was definitely not a date.

One night with a bit of dancing and some entertainment would do her a world of good.

She rummaged in the pocket of her pannier and pulled out some money. Folding it neatly, she pressed it into the pocket of her dress, gave her hair one last poke of submission and headed down to the kitchen.

Nicki was leaning in the doorway, her back to Sarah. As she brought a beer bottle to her lips and leaned back to take a swig, Sarah spotted Michael leaning against the kitchen table. She stopped in her tracks. He was dressed in jeans—clean, neat jeans that rested at his hips with a thick leather belt. His white cotton shirt was tucked in, all the way around, the sleeves rolled casually to just below his elbows, revealing his firm tanned forearms. The top two buttons were undone revealing tight curls of dark hair peeking from the V. She dragged her gaze up to his face and was greeted with a melting smile. He'd trimmed his beard and his face above it was smooth. It didn't have the polished glow of Amir's pampered skin; Michael's face looked fresh and clean and kissable.

Sarah flushed. Maybe this had been a bad idea. What if she was giving out the wrong vibe? What if this attraction was more than just, yeah, you're nice looking? And what if he picked up on that? What if he *acted* on it? What if Nicki accused her of leading him on, only to stomp on his heart, like Caroline had? Maybe she should fake a headache and go quietly back upstairs.

"Here she is," said Nicki, breaking through the crackle of electricity that was most definitely in the room.

"Hi," said Sarah, looking up into Michael's face. His look made the bones in her legs dissolve and she reached for the door frame to steady herself. Definitely should have faked the headache.

"You look lovely," he said.

"My girl dress." She pulled out the sides of her dress, like a six-year-old would, dropping them again immediately because that felt an awful lot to her like flirting. She definitely wasn't going to flirt.

"It's very becoming."

"Thank you," she said, feeling herself blush. "You clean up quite nicely yourself."

"Thank you," he said, pulling out the side of his jeans.

"Oh, for crying out loud, you two," said Nicki, laughing. "Cut it out."

Sarah blushed.

"Come on," said Michael, brushing past Nicki and guiding Sarah toward the door. "We don't need to stick around here to be insulted. I'm sure we can find better insults somewhere else." He held out his elbow in mock gallantry for Sarah to take. She hesitated for the tiniest fraction of a second. Was he flirting?

Of course he wasn't. He was joking around with his sister. That was all. She hooked her arm into the crook of his, playing along with his tease, and they marched together out of the kitchen door and into the night air.

But when they reached the street and the gag was over, she didn't pull her arm away and Michael didn't make a move to let her go. Her arm felt good against his side and she tried not to pay attention to how it felt for his body to rub against it, the muscles of his torso flexing and contracting as he walked. Oh God. She needed to pull her arm away. She really ought to pull her arm away. All she'd have to do was slide it out, ease it along his ribs, pay no attention to the ripple of his muscles as her skin slid along them.

Okay, stop, she thought. Stop this right now. She tensed her arm trying with every fiber of it to hold it perfectly still.

"To the fair!" yelled Nicki, practically rolling out the front door with Jennie behind her.

"Your sister's hilarious," Sarah said, searching for something to break the silence.

"Nicki? Yeah, she's about as subtle as a ton of bricks, but her heart's in the right place."

"You're lucky to have family close by."

"You know?" said Michael. "I am."

As the little group jostled down the lane toward the village green, Sarah's thoughts drifted to Luke. She missed her brother suddenly, wished she'd made more of an effort to see him. But he traveled so much for work and they never seemed to be in the same place at the same time. They talked when they could and he'd been the first person she'd told when she decided to call off the wedding. The thought that he might already have bought a ticket and that she'd be responsible for wasting it had almost been enough to change her mind about canceling. But when she'd called Luke, he'd seemed almost nonchalant about the whole thing. No, he hadn't bought his ticket yet and no, he didn't think she was an idiot for calling it off if she thought it was best. She'd been grateful when he hadn't asked if she'd chosen another date or when she thought it might be. She was glad to not feel that pressure from him, but it wasn't until after she'd said goodbye and put down the phone, telling Luke she'd see him soon, that she realized he wasn't planning to come to the wedding. It was as if he'd assumed the wedding would never happen.

As they got closer to the center of the village, the sound of music drifted their way. An accordion, was that? And bells?

"Morris dancers!" Sarah cried. She pulled Michael by the arm and dragged him to a gap in the crowd so she could watch the performance. She craned her neck, trying to see around the people in front, until she felt Michael's hands slip round her waist as he maneuvered her in front of him. She tried to focus on the dancers, listening to the accordion music, the jingle of bells and the clack of sticks. She knew it wasn't cool to love Morris dancers but she didn't care. Except right now she couldn't concentrate. She wondered how long a person could hold her breath without causing permanent damage. Probably not as long as she should. But if she breathed out now, her ribs would deflate, her waist would expand and Michael's hands would press closer to her. She wanted to feel that, but she couldn't take the risk.

As Michael shifted his weight in the crowd, his leg slid up against hers. His muscles were firm inside those well-worn jeans. He had an overall feeling of solidness that came from more than just his work-strong body. Amir had a beautiful body, lean limbs and skin that was almost silken. He worked hard on appearance and the results were, how would you say it? *Effective.* His skin called out to be touched, enjoyed, indulged in, and she had. But there was always a feeling of eating a decadent dessert, one of those creamy chocolate mousse things that made you sigh with every nibble. You could survive on chocolate mousse, certainly, and it would be a delicious way to live, but you wouldn't live for long and there was always that feeling with Amir of something insubstantial that couldn't last forever. And so she'd found ways to make it last, to hold on and enjoy the pleasure as long as she could. But somewhere along the way she'd lost herself. She'd stopped feeling nourished by their relationship. Instead she felt as if she'd tried to live on chocolate mousse—full, indulged, and satisfied but somehow empty, like she needed something more, something simple, like a cheese sandwich and a big mug of tea. Something comforting. Something more like Michael.

At last the dancers did their final jingling fanfare and the crowd dispersed. Sarah felt Michael move away from her and she let out her breath, both relieved and disappointed that the connection was broken.

"Uncle Mikey!" The shrill voices of two children rang out and Michael was gone.

When she turned, she found him crouched, collecting two bouncing children in his arms. He scooped them up, pushing up in a smooth powerful move, as if he were lifting two bags of flour.

Sarah wasn't good with children's ages, but she'd have to guess the girl was about nine, the little boy maybe seven. They clung to their uncle, their faces lit with absolute glee. Michael's head bobbed from one to the other, as he accepted kisses and listened to their excited stories.

Sarah had a fleeting flash of a memory, of she and Luke, spinning in their father's arms. It had been summertime. She could see her cotton dress and Luke's eternally grubby t-shirt, smell the faint tang of perspiration on her father, the smell of the sea in the air. They'd been at their grandmother's house, another summer spent waiting to see where they'd end up next. Their dad had come to visit, taken the train from wherever he had planted his own shallow roots. And Sarah had known this time he was back. She could remember that feeling of safety of knowing that finally everything was going to be okay. And then her dad had set them down, and said…

"This is my friend. Sarah."

Sarah snapped back to the present, back to the fair, back to Michael and the two children who were now examining her with a mix of curiosity and expectation, as if they thought she might sprout an extra head.

"It's very nice to meet you," she said, extending her hand for them to shake it.

For a moment, she was sure it was a wrong move. That woman had done the same thing, that woman who had stolen her dad. Her father had stepped aside and introduced a woman they hadn't noticed in their excitement.

"This is my friend. Shawna," he'd said. "Say hello."

Sarah and Luke had stared at the woman—Shawna. They'd taken in her short stretchy skirt and pale veined legs, the too-tight top into which she had stuffed her breasts. Sarah had been too young to fully understand the nature of the relationship between her dad and what their grandmother referred to as his "fancy woman", but she knew that Shawna, if she was a "friend" of her dad's, was a special sort of friend, a threatening sort of friend.

Her instincts were proven right when, after dinner that night, her dad and Shawna had left. She'd asked Grandma Lily when Daddy would be coming back for them, but her grandmother had sent them to bed. Later, she'd brought up warm milk and some bread and jam and explained to Sarah that Dad had some things he had to do and that he'd asked Grandma Lily to take care of her and Luke. When she asked for Sarah's help looking after Luke, Sarah said she would. That had been the last time she had seen her dad...ever.

Lost in her memories, Sarah didn't notice the small warm hand that had slipped into hers.

"My name's George," said the boy. "Mum says you rode your bike here all the way from London. Is that true?"

"It is," Sarah said.

George's eyes opened so wide they practically filled his face. "That's so cool," he said.

"Hello, Sarah," said the girl. "I'm Madison. Will you take us on the Ferris Wheel? Uncle Mikey's afraid of heights."

Sarah glanced at Michael, who shrugged and nodded. "What can I say? I'm more chicken than my chickens."

"I'd love to," Sarah said, and suddenly both her hands were filled with the hands of two very excited children. In the space of about ten seconds, she felt more a part of this family than she'd ever felt in her life. It was a feeling she liked a lot.

CHAPTER TWELVE

MICHAEL WAVED to his niece and nephew as their pod passed the top of its circle. Fearless. They were utterly fearless. He wished he could be up there with them, looking down on the village, the people he knew so well milling about like ants. He'd love to see the view of the valley and the surrounding hills. It would be like flying, like being a bird swooping over the landscape. Pity he was so petrified of heights. It all came down to trust, really. He could blame Caroline for damaging that.

As the pod swooped down, Sarah waved to him, a look of absolute joy and childlike abandon on her face. God, she was gorgeous. Did she have any idea?

He hadn't been himself since he'd wandered into Nicki's kitchen that morning and seen those smooth brown legs and those ridiculous sock lines. He'd pegged her right away as trouble, way too much work to handle, but he'd been wrong about her. For all her outward appearance of being above it all, he wasn't sure he'd ever met such a down-to-earth woman. His sister loved her, his niece and nephew had taken to her instantly. For Pete's sake, even his chickens had welcomed her into the roost. She was about as perfect a woman as he could hope to find.

Except for that one small detail: the fiancé.

Michael had the feeling that something wasn't right there, but he was hard pressed to put his finger on it.

"Penny for your thoughts?"

He turned to find his sister, Kate, peeking out at him from behind an enormous stuffed fish.

"Just watching your children for you. Nice fish."

"Dan won it for me on the hook-a-duck. For the number of tries he took, he could have bought it, but he was determined to win it for me. He's such a silly romantic sometimes."

Michael smiled at the twinkle in Kate's eyes. She was a smaller, quieter version of Nicki, the more reserved of the three siblings, but she was like a gushing teenager when she talked about Dan. From the second she'd clapped eyes on him it had been Dan this and Dan that. She had driven Michael to the brink of insanity twittering on about him, and everyone knew long before Kate did that the two of them would end up together. You could see it in her eyes.

That was it. That's what was missing with Sarah.

When she talked about Amir, there was something guarded about her. Her eyes didn't light up, she didn't gush about him endlessly. She talked about her bike with more passion than she talked about Amir. She used all the right words for a person talking about the man she was planning to marry, but that love and passion didn't quite have the strength to make it to her eyes. He wondered if she even realized. Perhaps she wasn't admitting to herself what was plain to everyone else: She was never going to marry Amir.

Michael knew one thing. He wasn't going to be the one to break the news to her.

The kids were bouncing around like baby kangaroos when they got off the Ferris wheel. They danced circles around Sarah, babbling about the ride and the fair.

"Guess what?" squealed Madison. "Sarah once jumped out of a plane."

"And she's lived in seventeen different houses," said George.

"And she rode all the way here on a bicycle named Cecelia."

"And someone stole it, but then Uncle Mikey tried to help her find it."

"He's her hero," swooned Madison.

Michael glanced at Sarah. Had she really said that? But she looked away. He took that to mean she had.

"I'm not telling you two any more of my secrets," Sarah said, trying to sound mad, but unable to keep the laughter out of her voice.

"I think you two need to burn off some energy. You're getting way too silly," said Kate. "Tell Sarah thank you for taking you on the scary ride."

Maddie and George launched themselves at Sarah, wrapping their arms around her and pressing themselves to her as if she were a Titanic life raft.

Michael wasn't much of an expert on kids, and Caroline had never shown much interest, but he had spent a lot of time with his growing niece and nephew and he understood one thing. Kids were fundamentally honest—often to a fault—and these kids thought Sarah was the bee's knees. He couldn't disagree.

"Fancy a beer?" he said to Sarah.

"Sounds like heaven," she said, and walked with him through the gathering crowd to find a spot in the beer garden.

The whole village had come out for the fair. Jennie was there, talking to Jamie's assistant Ollie, no doubt about the drama society's next production. Old Mrs. Belmont had settled at a table outside the cake tent where she could hold court with everyone who passed. She waved at Sarah as they passed, as if they knew one another. The vicar was lobbing beanbags at a row of coconuts, foolishly believing he could win a prize. They found a small table away from the music and Michael brought over two tall, cool beers. They sipped in silence, watching as Nicki found Jennie and pulled her onto the dance floor that had been laid in front of the main stage. Nicki was a maniac, arms flailing, hair flying around her until it stuck to her face with sweat.

Kate passed by at one point, a smear of dirt on her cheek from where she'd fallen, narrowly missing winning the sack race. When the adult three legged race was announced, Sarah grabbed Michael's hand and signed them up. They zipped down the field in perfect synchrony, striding over the line ahead of everyone else and collapsing in a heap of glory.

Just as the breeze coming from the valley started to turn chilly, a bonfire was lit at the far edge of the field and people took their drinks to get warm and watch the flames dance.

"You want to go over?" Michael said.

Sarah gazed at him through sleepy eyes, looking so relaxed he was worried she might slide into sleep right there. Was he that interesting? "I'm perfectly happy right here," she said patting the edge of her wooden stool.

And so was Michael. Perfectly happy, that is. He was in his favorite place in the world, his family and friends all around him, and this woman, this beautiful, funny, fearless, chicken-whispering woman sitting beside him. He could have stayed there all night.

"You want another drink?" he asked. "Bar's empty."

Sarah shook her head. "I think I've had enough. I could do with a walk, wake myself up a bit."

"I know the perfect place, and tonight's the perfect night to see it."

He took Sarah's hand and led her away from the fire. She didn't pull away. How long had it been since he'd held hands with a woman? Not since Caroline and even then, had they ever held hands? "I think we're a little old for that, don't you?" Caroline always said. He'd agreed, because he supposed it did seem childish, but holding Sarah's hand now, he realized he'd been wrong.

He'd forgotten the special kind of heat that radiates from one person's hand to another's. He thought you could tell a lot by the way someone held your hand. He squeezed a little more and tried to sense the message he was picking up from Sarah. He couldn't quite pinpoint it, but a spark of excitement and adventure jumped from her to him. She seemed content, had been energized since the three-legged race, laughter bubbling from her. He sensed no hesitation as they stepped away from the noise of the fair.

"Where are we going?" she said, after a while. Her voice still held a tinkle of laughter.

"It's a bit of a hike, but I promise you it's worth it."

"Well, I'm tired from all that running so you're going to have to pull me if it's up hill."

She sounded a little tipsy, but he'd had a couple of the local brews, too, and he was feeling giddy. "Come on," he said, hunkering down and spreading his arms to catch her. "I'll give you a piggy back."

"I'm too heavy," she said, even as she wrapped her arms around his neck and jumped.

He felt his knees buckle as she mounted his back, but it

had nothing at all to do with her weight. Her legs, those long, lean legs, wrapped around his waist. Her muscles were strong and they gripped tightly around him, their power almost taking his breath away. She pressed herself close to him and he relished the tickle of the stray tendrils of her hair brushing against his ear and the warmth of her breath on his neck.

When she laughed, it reverberated through her body and into his. A lustful groan climbed up through his chest. He pushed it down before it could escape. He didn't want to break this little spell of utterly blissful heaven.

"I'm not too heavy, am I?" she said again.

"For a big, strong man like me? No way."

She laughed again and his body shook. He wanted to keep her laughing forever.

"Giddy up, pony," she yelled and urged him forward, thrusting herself against him. He wasn't sure he had the wherewithal to maintain his decorum. He set off at a trot, partly to play along with her game and partly to outrun the lustful feelings that were taking over him.

He was close to dying by the time they reached the top of the hill. A rivulet of sweat trickled down his back and his lungs heaved in his chest. He was glad the light was starting to dim so Sarah couldn't see how red his face was. Maybe he wasn't quite as fit as he'd thought the country life had made him.

When they reached a small wooden gate, he stopped to let Sarah dismount, leaving his back feeling cold where her body slipped away from his. He wanted the feeling back right away. Instead, he opened the gate and ushered her through.

"Where are we going?" she asked again.

He grinned. "You are so impatient."

"I just don't like surprises, that's all."

He frowned at her. "Who doesn't like surprises?"

"I've had way too many in my lifetime and most of them weren't good."

Her eyes darkened. There was so much she wasn't telling him, but he was afraid if he asked now, this small sliver of bliss they'd been enjoying would be lost. Instead, he took her hand, glad for the small point of contact, and led her to the very crown of the hill where the ground leveled out. Around the top stood a ring of stones. "There," he said at last.

"It's a stone circle," she said. "I've read about these. All sorts of strange magical things are supposed to happen inside them."

She let go of his hand and danced between the stones, spinning with her arms flung out. God, she was lovely. She stopped at a stone about three feet tall and ran her hand over it. "It's Midsummer. Aren't we supposed to dance naked or something?" she said.

Michael blinked, unable to speak. He had a fleeting vision of Sarah's smooth silken legs and what was attached above them. Dancing naked in the stone circle sounded like exactly what he had in mind. "Well," he said, trying not to sound too enthusiastic for the idea. "You can if you want."

She reached behind her as if to unbutton her dress. Michael stared, unable to believe what was about to happen. She gave him a provocative look that zinged right to the bit of himself he was fighting hard to control. Just as all the moisture evaporated from his mouth, she dropped her hands and looked at him. "Right," she said. "Do you think I'm going to strip naked up here and end up on the front page of the village newspaper next weekend?"

He shut his mouth, which he now realized, to his

embarrassment, had been hanging open. It's a wonder his tongue hadn't been lolling out, too.

The midsummer sky was a bluish peach, the shade unique to a sky the sun can't quite leave behind.

"You can see for miles up here," Sarah said. "It's beautiful."

"Bit different from London, isn't it?" Michael said.

Sarah murmured, which he took to be a yes. "I can see why you came back," she said at last, moving toward him. "Do you ever regret it?"

"No," he said. "Never."

"Even when your chickens won't lay?"

"Nope."

"Even when it's freezing cold and you still have to go outside because there's no one else to do it."

"Not even then."

"Even when you go to bed at nine o'clock because there's nothing else to do but watch TV."

"Nope."

"Even when you're lonely and there's nothing you can do about it because you're stubbornly determined to do this alone to prove something to someone for some reason?"

He didn't answer. She was wrong. That wasn't what this was all about at all. He wasn't doing this to prove a point. He wasn't doing this to show that he didn't need anyone. "This has nothing to do with Caroline," he said.

"I didn't say it did."

He opened his mouth to argue, but she'd caught him.

CHAPTER THIRTEEN

SARAH LAY on her back in the center of the stone circle, her whole body softened by the beers they'd drunk. Beside her, Michael plucked at the grass. The wavering sound of music drifted up from the village, ebbing and flowing as the wind carried the sound toward them. In the lulls, the silence lapped over them, interrupted by the occasional twittering of a bird heading in for the evening. Sarah gazed out across the moors fading now into the late pink glow of evening. She loved the way the light changed as the day went on, highlighting the colors of the heather, the trees, the grass. Maybe before she left she would come up here in the early morning, watch the sun rise over the village. Maybe Michael would come with her.

For the first time in a long time, Sarah felt alive. Away from the confines of Amir's family and the expectations of her behavior, she could be herself and she was surprised to find that who she was wasn't who she'd expected. She liked this Sarah.

She played back the events of the evening, relishing again the simple joy of the evening spent with Michael and his family. She pictured Nicki with her hair stuck to her face from hours of non-stop dancing, the smear of dirt on Kate's cheek where she'd taken a tumble in the sack race. She tried to imagine Claudette climbing into an old potato sack and jumping down the length of a field for fun. Claudette and fun weren't two things that often went together.

She thought then about flying through the air with Madison and George. That was the thing that was sticking in her chest. In the future life she'd so carefully mapped out, would she ever ride a fairground ride with her children and laugh like she'd laughed tonight? Would Amir ever take her by the hand and give her a piggy back up to a stone circle at the top of a hill? So much about her life with Amir was safe and comfortable, what she'd thought she always wanted. But tonight she had felt the opposite, free and a little reckless, but instead of scaring her, it had felt good.

Could I live this life? she thought. *This unstable, scary, wonderful life?*

Michael had been quiet for a while and she turned to see if he was mesmerized by the light too. But he wasn't. He was hunched over, working intently on something in his hands.

"What are you doing?" she asked.

He didn't respond at first and she wondered if he'd heard her, then he looked up and smiled. It was such a lovely boyish grin and it made her tickle inside.

"I made you a present," he said, then suddenly looked coy. He held out the thing he'd been so focused on and she saw it was a long thin loop: a daisy chain. She laughed and Michael seemed suddenly embarrassed. He started to put it down, but she leaned forward, ducking her head.

"It's silly," he said.

"No. I love it."

He smiled again and it filled his entire face. She felt the glow of it transmit into her. He leaned in and placed the necklace of flowers around her neck. She arranged it so it fell neatly down the front of her dress. When she looked back up he hadn't moved. His face was inches from hers and before she could stop herself, she leaned in and kissed him.

His lips grazed hers and the electricity of his kiss ran all the way down from her lips to her legs. A soft moan escaped from her mouth and when Michael pulled her toward him, she didn't resist. As they sank back on the grass, her entire body melted against his, every fiber zinging with longing. She ran her hands down his chest, feeling his muscles tense at her touch. And then her hands met his belt, found the folds of his shirt and freed it from his jeans. She slid her palm under the pressed white cotton and touched his skin. He groaned and pressed against her leg. Her body seemed to disappear into his and he pulled her closer.

When he leaned away, she read everything he was saying in his eyes. He got to his feet and took her hand. And when he pulled her to her feet and led her silently back down into the village, she went along. She didn't object when he took a path away from the festivities of the fair and toward his cottage. And when he led her up the creaky wooden stairs that led to his bedroom, she didn't object at all.

CHAPTER FOURTEEN

SARAH STRETCHED her arm across the sheets, feeling the comforting scratch of well-loved fabric across her skin. She stretched each part of her exhausted body, feeling each muscle's reluctant spark of life. She tried to roll her head to stretch her neck, but the weight of it pressed into the pillow and it refused to move. She groaned and tried to open her eyes, but the faint glow of morning sun through the curtains felt like another nail pinning her dull head to the bed.

I will never drink again, she thought. It must be the ale from the beer garden that had hit her. She'd only had a couple, but they had gone down so smoothly, quenching her thirst from the warm evening air. They had soothed her soul and fueled the joy she had felt at being a kid again. Riding the Ferris Wheel, cheering on the silly contests, taking a piggy back to the stone circle. Climbing onto Michael's back. Wrapping her legs around his body. Holding his hand and following him down the hill and up to—

She shot up in bed. Her weary brain knocked against the inside of her skull as she opened her eyes to the evil glaring sunlight. Plain blue curtains, a tall wooden dresser, jeans in a rumpled heap on the floor. Men's jeans. She ran her hand over the sheets. Blue checked flannel, pilled from countless washings, a vague scent of something warm and tangy embedded into the fabric.

Michael's bedroom. Michael's bed. Oh God. What had she done?

The sheets were rumpled and her pillow was indented from the weight of her heavy head. The other pillow lay at an angle, squashed into an hourglass shape, as if it had been hugged. Michael's shirt—the one he had worn to the fair—was folded neatly over the back of a chair. Her cotton dress hung from a hanger on the back of the wardrobe door. Had they undressed with such precision, or had Michael got up early and cleared up the debris of their night of passion?

She was wearing a thin gray t-shirt with Hope Valley Young Farmers barely visible in faded lettering on the front. She was wearing underwear, her underwear. She scanned her body, searching for evidence of what exactly had transpired the night before but she could find no clues, except for the puffiness in her lips and the soreness around her chin that she assumed was caused by the chafe of a beard.

She dropped her head into her hands. All this talk about loving Michael's solid family, all this big idea about taking a trip to find herself. Oh, she'd found herself okay, and what she'd found was that she was her father's daughter: unreliable, a liar, a cheat.

She eased her weary body out of bed and padded barefoot across the wood floor. With a sense of dread weighing down her legs, she went downstairs to find out what level of mess she had gotten herself into. She was pretty sure it was high.

Someone was in the kitchen. She hoped it was Michael. The smell of fresh coffee reached her nose and she followed its tantalizing fingers into the kitchen. Michael was dressed like he had already been outside. On the roughhewn kitchen table was a basket of eggs.

"Morning," he said when he heard her behind him. "Sleep okay?"

She nodded. "You?"

"I think that couch poked a spring in me all night, but aside from that, yes."

Sarah glanced back into the living room. Sure enough, a fluffy quilt was folded at the foot of the couch with a pillow stacked on top. "You slept on the couch?" she asked.

"Of course."

Michael smiled at her and her heart filled up faster than the coffee mug he was holding beneath the spout of a French press. He'd slept on the couch. Sarah's brief disappointment was quickly replaced by relief. He had been a complete gentleman. And she had not let herself down after all. At least not entirely.

She sank into the nearest chair and accepted the mug of coffee from Michael. Snippets of the evening came back to her now. The feel of her hand in Michael's, his lips covering hers, the scent of his body pressed close, the feel of his skin under her hands. The night had not been completely innocent.

"You look worried," he said. "Are you okay?"

She thought about his question and shook her head. She was not okay. She'd called off the wedding because it wasn't the wedding she'd wanted. But now she'd put the whole marriage in doubt. She'd been so happy here in this imperfect world. Maybe she'd gone to the stone circle with Michael because she was tipsy, but that's not why she'd gone home with him. She'd gone home with him because he felt real—not safe and solid like Amir, but real. She knew then that she couldn't marry Amir.

"I need to go," she said.

Michael looked surprised. "Well, at least have some breakfast first."

"I don't mean go now. And yes, I'm starving; breakfast would be amazing. I mean I need to leave, go back to London, deal with my life."

"Oh," Michael said.

She pushed back from the table and moved toward him. "Not forever," she said.

"What will you do after that?"

"I don't know yet," she said and a cold fear gripped her. If she didn't marry Amir, what would she do? "Go back to my job. Put my life back together, I suppose."

"Will you come back?" Michael asked.

She had no idea and her brain didn't have the space to work that out yet. One thing at a time, and the first thing on her list was to be honest with Amir. Forget the bike, forget the ride. She needed to go home. But would she come back?

She nodded.

Michael looked at her and his face softened and melted into the biggest smile. He pulled her toward him wrapping his arms around her. "I'd like that," he said. And then he kissed her like he really meant it.

Maybe she could stay a little while longer.

After two mugs of coffee and some fresh eggs courtesy of the fruitful ladies, Michael took her by the hand and led her outside. "I have something to show you," he said. "I was going to wait because it's not quite ready, but now seems like as good a time as any."

Sarah giggled. "I can hardly wait."

"It's not a big deal," he said. "Well, it *is* a big deal, it's just not anything special. Well, it's special, but not... Oh, never mind. Just come with me."

He led her to the barn behind the farmhouse. Sarah had visions of haylofts and rolling but she pushed them from her mind. Michael opened the heavy wooden door and Sarah blinked in the semi-darkness.

"Hold on," Michael said, and flicked on a light.

Now she could see a workbench and tools hung on a peg board. A half-finished wooden box stood on the bench beside a roll of chicken wire, some indeterminate project yet to be completed. And in the middle of the floor was a bike. It had a scratched purple frame and a mismatched set of wheels. The saddle was worn but made from good quality leather. A Brooks. She recognized it.

"Is this yours?" she asked.

"No." Michael grinned. "It's yours."

She didn't understand at first. This wasn't like Cecelia at all, not even close.

"I called back around the calling tree to check on your bike," Michael said, "and you'd be amazed how many people had bike parts lying around. It's not quite ready but I couldn't wait any longer. I know it's not much, but at least you could maybe finish your ride on it."

Sarah stared at the bike, her heart thudding in her chest. It was the strangest mismatched contraption she had ever seen, but it was everything. It was her freedom again, an act of kindness from strangers, all of it. But most of all it meant that Michael had listened to her and heard what she'd said. And even though the bike meant she would be able to leave, he was willing to let her go.

"Thank you," she said, and threw her arms around his neck.

"I'll be sorry to see you go, but maybe you'll come back."

"Will you be here if I do?"

"Right here," he said and laid his fingers on her chest.

For the rest of the morning and into the afternoon, she and Michael worked in the garden, stopping only briefly to eat lunch together. As the sun began its dip toward the top of the hills, Sarah wrapped her hand around a thick purple stem and tugged. The soil cracked and fell away and a beautiful round beet emerged, towing a long tail of roots behind it. She dusted off the heaviest of the mud and laid it in the basket. She was already envisioning a grated beet salad, with a simple balsamic dressing and giant brick of cheese, courtesy of the goats. She glanced down the row to where Michael was turning over the soil in preparation for a winter crop of potatoes. He caught her looking and beamed at her. God, he was beautiful. As she bent to pick the next beet, something glinting in the distance caught her eye. She turned, still daydreaming about food and Michael, to see what it was.

At first, there was nothing in the spot where she'd first seen the flash, but as she began to look away, she saw it again, lower down the hill. It had to be a car, and even though she couldn't see it, she felt a cold dread pass through her. She shook it off. Just her mind playing tricks on her, but she found herself edging toward the cover of the blackberry bushes to a spot she wouldn't easily be seen from the road. A few minutes later, a sleek midnight blue Jaguar slid into view and glided, almost silently, through the village.

Sarah pressed herself into the bushes, yelping as a tendril of thorny blackberry branch caught against her cheek. The car stopped outside Nicki's, a chauffeur held open the door, and a man climbed out. He straightened his long body and dusted down his jacket. He glanced both ways down the street, taking in the village and then stepped to the door of the Sunnydale B&B.

"What's all this lollygagging, woman," said Michael, grinning as he strode through the garden bearing two steaming mugs of tea. "Don't you know there's work to be done?"

His face fell as he looked beyond her and spotted the car. "Looks like Nicki's got a visitor, but it doesn't look like a friendly call. Looks a bit official."

"Yes," mumbled Sarah, taking the tea and focusing on it to avoid catching Michael's eye.

"Looks like a detective or the government. Hope she's not in trouble."

Sarah said nothing.

"I wonder if I should go over and see if she's okay?" he said.

Sarah tried to speak. She knew she needed to say something, but nothing she could think of would have a good outcome.

"Actually," she said finally. "I think he's looking for me."

For a moment, Michael looked at her as if he was trying to work out if she was a hardened criminal on the lam or a tax dodger. Then something seemed to click and Sarah could almost see the lightbulb go off in his head as he put together the pieces of the puzzle and understood that the visitor was Amir.

"Ah," he said. "I see." He took the mug out of Sarah's hand, but didn't look up. His voice was quiet when he next spoke. "I suppose you'd better be going then."

Sarah couldn't speak. She wanted to apologize or to explain or to tell Michael something—not to worry or that it wasn't important. But none of that was true and they both knew it. She'd been fooling herself with this playing at the country life and she realized now, to her chagrin, that she'd been fooling Michael too. She'd made a big mistake.

CHAPTER FIFTEEN

EVEN FROM JUST INSIDE the front door, Sarah could hear the laughter coming from the kitchen. She heard Jennie's shy, tinkling giggle and Nicki's round, bobbing laugh. And beneath them was the deep confident rumble of Amir's voice.

He was charming his audience, as only Amir knew how. He'd have said something witty, complimented Nicki on something, not her hair or her appearance, not something trivial. He'd have told her how much he loved what she'd done with the old stone cottage, or admired the welcoming coziness of the kitchen. He'd have sussed out immediately what held the strings of Nicki's heart and he'd have struck right to the core.

Listen to me, thought Sarah. I'm talking about him like he's a snake. And he wasn't like that at all. He was always genuine with his compliments, he'd never tell a lie for the sake of flattery, but he had a way of delivering his charm that disarmed even the wiliest person.

"The secret," Nicki was saying as Sarah reached the door, "is the tiniest pinch of nutmeg."

Amir held a piece of cake under his long, aquiline nose and sniffed. "Nutmeg. Of course. It's utterly divine."

Nicki beamed at him, her smile slipping only for an instant when she spotted Sarah in the doorway.

"Here she is," she said to Amir, the smile springing back onto her face. As Amir turned, Nicki shot Sarah a look that Sarah interpreted as "My, oh my, you have a lot of explaining to do." She would have noticed that Sarah had missed breakfast that morning, perhaps assumed, surmised, or otherwise discovered that her bed had not been slept in, and that Michael's had. Had she jumped to the obvious, but wrong, conclusion? Had she hinted to Amir that his fiancée had been otherwise engaged?

Sarah watched Amir's gaze flit over her and in that infinitesimal instant she saw him take in her grubby clothes, her disheveled hair, the faint aroma of dirt that seemed to follow her around. And perhaps he sensed her guilt too.

"Well, this is a nice surprise," she beamed. No guilt; she'd done nothing wrong. Her mind flashed briefly to Michael's bedroom. A simple mistake, but there was no crime in sleeping alone in a stranger's bed. No crime at all, unless you'd lingered long enough to take in the scent that hung in the air, or cast your eyes at the pile of discarded clothes and imagined him taking them off, or if you'd pictured what he'd look like stretched out on that vast expanse of bed wrapped in nothing but your legs. Okay, then there might be reason for a smidge of guilt.

"I was beginning to worry you'd been abducted," he said, his creamy voice lapping over the words.

"No," she laughed.

"Nicki here's been telling me about your escapades. If I'd known I'd have come sooner."

She glanced at Nicki, trying to gauge what exactly she'd

been telling Amir. She caught a slight shake of Nicki's head, enough to let her know she'd given Amir only the humorous snippets of the tale of the stolen bike, and a look that said, "And you owe me."

"Let me get cleaned up and we'll go to the pub for a bite and a pint," Sarah said to Amir. "I'll tell you all about it there."

"I already have reservations. My treat."

Sarah knew what "reservations" meant to Amir, and it wasn't throwing on jeans and ambling to the pub for a shepherd's pie and a Guinness. "I don't have anything fancy to wear."

Amir cocked his head to one side, "Of course," he said. "I took the liberty. I'll have Jacques bring in the bag."

He stood and leaned into her, hesitating for a moment as if looking for a clean patch of skin on which to land a kiss. Finding none, he kissed the air by her temple. "Funny girl," he said, shaking his head as if dismayed by what he saw, and he glided from the room as if on an invisible conveyor belt.

No one in the kitchen said a word as they watched him go. Sarah's insides churned as she tried to sort through the feelings that tumbled through her. When she turned back to the kitchen, Nicki and Jennie were watching her, their mouths pursed in anticipation of her explanation.

"That's Amir," Sarah said, dumbly.

"So he said," said Nicki, in what Sarah thought was a rather acerbic tone.

"My fiancé," Sarah added.

"He made a point of mentioning that, actually."

Sarah flushed.

"He's really nice looking," said Jennie. "He looks like he's loaded. Did you see that car? 'I took the liberty,'" she said, doing a shockingly accurate imitation of Amir. "'I'll have Jacques bring in your bag.' Bloody hell. And there's you giving it, 'Oh, let's go down to the pub.' You must be joking."

"Well," said Nicki, pushing back from the table and gathering the tea things. "Much as I'd love to sit around discussing Prince Charming, I've got work to do. Need to prep for the morning and take a loaf down for my *brother*." She gave Sarah a strained smile as she emphasized "brother."

"Nicki," said Sarah, but Nicki waved her off.

"Have a nice evening and *perhaps* I'll see you in the morning." And she turned and left, leaving Sarah feeling like something unpleasant that got stuck under someone's shoe.

In her room, Sarah unzipped the bag that Jacques had carried up for her. She knew it wouldn't just contain clothes and shoes. There'd be perfume, stockings, make-up, even hair products. Amir would have thought of everything, or at least instructed one of his staff to think of everything. She knew men who would pick out their wife's clothes, dictate the length of her hair, and oversee all aspects of her life. But Amir wasn't like that. He wouldn't have packed *his* favorite dress, he would have brought *hers*, the one she always felt comfortable in, probably the blue wraparound one that she always joked would stretch with her meal. He would have made reservations at a restaurant he knew she'd love and he'd have checked (or had his assistant, check) that the chef could offer a selection of healthy options. In other words, he'd treat her like royalty, offer her everything any woman would long for just once. And so why did she wish he'd never come?

She suddenly understood why Nicki had been so sharp with her. A runaway bride flirting harmlessly with her brother was one thing; a woman with a flesh-and-blood fiancé spending the night at her brother's house—no matter what had or hadn't happened between them—was an entirely different kettle of fish.

Sarah felt strangely uncomfortable in the blue dress she had guessed Amir had chosen. The fabric seemed to cling and the snug waist felt restrictive. Her face felt smothered under the layer of make-up and her hair felt like a hairspray helmet in the tight chignon she'd assembled. The only evidence that an hour ago she'd been up to her knuckles in beets was a stubborn speck of dirt that refused to budge from beneath the nail of her ring finger.

Her ring finger! Had Amir noticed that she wasn't wearing her ring? She rummaged in her drawer and pulled out the diamond, slipping it onto her finger, where it immediately spun upside-down. She set it straight and checked herself one last time in the mirror. Staring back was a woman she no longer knew, a woman who had chosen her path, only to realize once she was deep into the woods, that she'd gone the wrong way. She patted her lipstick and stared herself dead in the eye. It was time to retrace her steps, back to the Sarah she used to be. She had to tell Amir the truth.

When she returned downstairs, Nicki and Jennie were nowhere to be seen. She was glad they hadn't seen her all dressed up like the woman she had once been. Amir gave her an approving smile and escorted her to the waiting car. As she ducked down into the back seat, she caught a glimpse of Michael's cottage. She said a silent thank you that he wasn't there to see her leave.

As they drove away, Sarah rested her head against the window and watched the dusky outlines of the trees flash by. She didn't ask where they were going. Amir had come with a plan and she no longer had the strength to argue with it or even to care much what it was. She'd listen to what he had to say and then she'd tell him everything. She wouldn't expect him to understand, but this time she would stand her ground.

"You look beautiful," Amir said, taking her hand and squeezing her fingers in his. "I'm sorry to surprise you, but you didn't answer my calls. I was worried."

"Your calls?" Sarah said. "When did you call?"

"I tried to reach you again last night, after we talked."

"I was at the fair. I didn't hear my phone."

"When you didn't return my call I tried again this morning."

Sarah frowned. How had she missed his call?

"I tried several times, actually," said Amir. "And when I couldn't reach you, I was worried. Is your phone not charged?"

"It should be," Sarah said reaching for the purse Amir had brought, but knowing the phone wouldn't be there. She'd been so flustered, she'd forgotten to switch it over from... From where? Where had she last seen her phone?

She felt the color drain from her face as she saw the phone clearly. The last place she'd seen it was on Michael's dresser. If he had found it, he would see that Amir had called.

She'd have to get the phone back in the morning. But was Amir planning to spend the night? She'd have to make an excuse to go to Michael's alone, maybe something about the chickens. Or maybe she could get a message to him via Nicki, assuming Nicki was still willing to do her a favor.

But truthfully, she wanted to see Michael again before she left. She wanted to tell him how courageous she thought he was to throw everything in and to take a chance on this lifestyle. How much she admired him for sticking to his guns even when things were hard. It was a ridiculous life he'd chosen for himself. She laughed to herself as she imagined the look on Amir's face—or even better, the look on Claudette's face—if she suddenly announced she was giving up her job, her London flat, and all the comforts that life with Amir afforded her, to live off the land, "just to prove she could."

"What's so funny?" Amir asked. Apparently she hadn't laughed to herself after all.

"Life," she said. "Life is funny sometimes, isn't it?"

Amir peered at her. "On the contrary," he said. "Life is the most serious thing of all."

CHAPTER SIXTEEN

MICHAEL HAD a bad feeling about Sarah's visitor. He wondered if he should go over and make sure she was okay. But Sarah was perfectly capable of taking care of herself; if she needed his help, she'd ask. He would take a shower, try to wash out the kinks after his night on the lumpy couch, but most of all, he'd give her space.

As he pulled open a drawer to find a clean shirt, he spotted Sarah's phone on the dresser. His first instinct was to run over and take it to her, but he didn't want to make an awkward scene in front of her visitor. He'd take his shower first and then go.

Michael let the hot water cascade over his head. He was just daydreaming about faeries and dust and circles of tiny, alluring Sarahs when his own phone rang. He finished rinsing off, wrapped a towel around his waist and took the call.

"Huh-lo," he growled, his voice tripping on the gravelly texture of his throat.

"Michael?"

The familiar voice zinged at a spot deep in his chest, but in his grogginess, it took him a moment to match the feeling of longing with the memory that had landed him in the past.

"Caroline," he said, as matter-of-factly as he could.

"You sound terrible," she said. "Are you sick?"

He tried to straighten out his jumbled thoughts. Was he sick? He groaned. No, not sick, something far worse than that. He was suffering from a bad case of something for which he needed to find a cure. He had the Sarahs.

"I'm fine," he said, his thoughts catching up to him again. Why was she ringing? They'd had little reason to communicate since their split, no family news they'd been obligated to share and thankfully, no lingering conflicts to hash around again. That had been one good thing about their parting; it had been quick and as amicable as it could have been for a public humiliation of epic proportions. But they hadn't dragged it out, hadn't bickered about possessions and who owed whom what. She'd just ripped out his heart, grilled it up with salt and pepper and served it back to him on a plate. No animosity there. So, now that she was calling, it had to be for something important.

"Are you all right?" he asked. He felt a sudden flicker of glee that perhaps she had called off the wedding. The glee was replaced immediately with guilt.

"I'm fine," she said. She paused and he heard a change in her tone. It had been a long time since he'd heard her like this but he recognized that light silkiness in her voice, the way she spoke when she was truly happy. God, it had been years since he'd heard it and it stirred up old feelings of longing for the time when their life together had been good, when he had been enough for her. "It's about the wedding," she said.

Michael's spirits lifted. So it hadn't worked out after all. "What about it?"

"Andy and I have been talking, and we think, under the circumstances, that it wouldn't be appropriate to invite you."

Michael was stunned. He hadn't expected an invitation and would have politely declined if he'd received one, but the idea of his ex-fiancée and his ex-friend suddenly deciding what was and wasn't appropriate stung more than a surprise invitation would have.

"I wanted to explain our rationale, rather than just exclude you," Caroline went on. "We made the right decision, didn't we?"

"You tell me," Michael said.

"I knew you'd understand. You always were reasonable."

"Always," Michael said, his tone flat.

"While I've got you on the phone I may as well tell you my other news. Better than hearing it through the grapevine."

Michael scoffed. The trusty grapevine was how he'd first learned of Caroline's affair. Now she wanted to be upfront with him? This was all too much. He gritted his teeth. "More news?" Wasn't a wedding enough? But he knew what was coming. He could feel it in the way his heart seemed to stretch with longing and sag with the impending news.

"I'm expecting," she said.

His heart reached its point of maximum sag and unable to stretch any further, it gave up and broke in two. "Oh," was all he could manage to say.

Caroline twittered on about how it was a surprise, not planned, but not unwanted. How they'd been so shocked at first and then ultimately ecstatic. She waffled about how she'd always dismissed those seemingly sensible women who went all mushy when they had babies but how she could already see how she would be exactly the same way when she saw her baby, oh, and how much she was looking forward to the challenges of motherhood.

Michael thought that human beings must have a switch that automatically clicked on in time of shock. He assumed that automatic part of him must have kept making appropriately suitable murmurs of approval because Caroline kept talking, so that the other part of him could get on with the important business of dying. Two years ago Caroline had whipped his life out from underneath him, taking all he thought he'd ever wanted. Now she was back to point out the rest of what she'd stolen: a family. He felt as if he was standing on a desert island watching the only ship to have come by in years sailing off into the sunset without him. Onboard was Caroline with a suitcase stuffed with his happiness, his life, and now his would-be children.

"I'm really happy for you," the automaton said.

Caroline stopped. "Oh, please don't be like that, Michael."

He snapped back to reality. "Like what?"

"Like, 'Oh, I'm so happy for you.'"

"Well, what do you want me to say?"

"I want you to be happy for me."

Now he was confused. "I just told you that I was."

"Yes, but you didn't mean it. I can tell by the way you said it."

"Should I have told you I wasn't happy so you'll know I really am? I mean, forgive me, Caroline, but this is a little tricky to get right."

Caroline sighed and he heard her voice crack. Now she

was going to cry? He wasn't sure exactly how he had messed this up, but tears were a sure sign that he had. "Oh Michael. I know I hurt you. I know I did. But we both know that I did the right thing. We could never have been happy together."

"That's funny," he said, "because I was actually sort of happy right up to the point that you decided we weren't."

"You have to let this go," Caroline said. "You're a good person, Michael, and you deserve a happy life. The thing I want more than anything is for you to find happiness again like I have."

Caroline. Never content to stick one knife in his chest, she had to stick in a second and twist them both, then beat him on the head with a cricket bat for good measure. "Well, you can't always get everything you want, Caroline. Life's just like that, so maybe you should be content with your new husband and your new baby and not be greedy by wanting my happiness too."

It was petulant, he knew it was, but honestly, she didn't really care whether he was happy or not; she just wanted to assuage her guilt. Well, bugger that. He hoped her guilt would give her indigestion. He hung up the phone, pulled on some clothes and stomped across the street to the comfort of his sister. Only when he was halfway there did he remember Sarah's phone and the visitor. Could this day get any worse?

Michael sat at the broad kitchen table while Nicki and Jennie buzzed around making welcome trays for the evening's newly-arrived guests. He poured his heart out about Caroline and already he was feeling better. It was over and he was better off without her. And then he asked about Sarah, and his sister told him about the visitor.

"Where did they go?" he asked as Nicki warmed a teapot.

"I don't know."

"Did she seem glad to see him?"

"I suppose so."

"What was he like?" Michael wasn't even sure why he was asking so many questions. Sarah's personal life was none of his business and it didn't matter what his sister thought about this Amir person. What mattered was what Sarah thought of him.

He admitted, if only to himself, that it was pretty childish of him to hope that Sarah had been annoyed by Amir's sudden arrival. Why wouldn't she be glad of a surprise visit from her fiancé? Why shouldn't she be thrilled to spend the night with the man she was going to marry. The bigger question was, why was he, Michael, in such a tangle over a woman engaged to another man? He could hear Jamie's voice in his head. "I mean, Michael, come on mate, talk about warning lights flashing." No good ever came from falling for someone else's fiancée. Someone totally unavailable.

"He was tall, dark, and handsome, wasn't he?" Michael said.

"No," said Nicki.

His head shot up. Maybe he'd envisioned this Amir fellow all wrong after all.

"He was average height, maybe a bit above, and he had dark hair, but his eyes were light colored, so not the swarthy dark you had in mind."

"Handsome?" Michael ventured.

Nicki shook her head and his hopes soared. "Actually, he wasn't so much handsome as devastatingly good-looking, charming, funny, and utterly likable. I can see why she, or anyone really, would fall for him. Not to mention he's richer than God. But classy, not flashy. He's pretty much the perfect package. I'd run off with him, given half a chance."

"Thanks," Michael said. "That's really made me feel better. What an amazing sister you turned out to be." He slumped in his chair, feeling utterly defeated.

"You need to tell her how you feel," said Nicki, sliding a mug of tea in front of him and arranging homemade cakes on china plates.

"How I feel about what?" he asked, playing dumb.

His sister shook her head at him. Why did he still try to get things by her when he knew she never missed a trick?

"She's engaged, in case you haven't noticed, Nicki. Totally, utterly unavailable."

"Which is why she's so attractive to you."

"What do you mean?"

"You've been playing this 'I don't need anyone' thing ever since Caroline left, but I know you well enough to know you're not going to just drop it. You don't want to admit you were wrong, that you made a mistake. So instead you go and fall hook, line, and sinker for someone you can't have. It's classic."

"I have not fallen hook, line, or sinker. I just think she's nice and yes, she's extremely attractive, and yes, I've enjoyed her being around here."

"And your eyes light up every time she comes within half a mile of you. And you turned up on my doorstep when I know you have about a million other things you could and should be doing. They are not the actions of a disinterested man, dear bro."

Michael harrumphed and took a long slug of his tea. It scorched the back of his throat and he felt it burn all the way down to his stomach. Sort of the way he'd felt when he'd kissed Sarah. Ugh. He'd kissed Sarah. Not a brilliant move on his part. But Sarah had kissed him too. Was that the action of a woman devoted to another man?

"Why don't you stay for dinner," Nicki said. "You can't go home with a broken heart and an empty stomach."

"I'm fine," he said. His stomach, the cheat, gave a traitorous growl.

"Bacon sandwich?"

He hesitated. "I'll pay you back."

"On the house."

"I don't need a sympathy feeding."

"Yes, you do," said Nicki. "So sit."

He ate the sandwich in silence, his thoughts folding over one another like the omelet Nicki was now tossing in a pan.

"She's not Caroline," he said at last.

"No," said Nicki. "She's human."

"You never liked Caroline, did you?"

"I never trusted her."

"And you were right." He drank the last of his tea. "Do you like Sarah?"

Nicki gave him a sly look. "Go home, get some rest, and get yourself back here first thing in the morning."

"For what?"

"For telling this woman how you feel before she's chauffeured out of your life and you never get the chance."

"I'll make a fool of myself."

"What's new?"

"What if she doesn't feel the same way?"

Nicki shrugged. "I'm no relationship expert, as we all know, but something's not right with those two. I'm not suggesting you storm in and break things up, but if you feel like I think you feel and she feels like I think she feels, you'll kick yourself for the rest of your life if you let her go."

Michael stared at his sister. What she was suggesting was crazy. And yet ... and yet ... a decision began to solidify. He would finish the bike tonight and bring it to her in the morning. He'd tell her in his own awkward way how he felt about her and, instead of letting her go, he'd say what he really meant. He'd ask her to stay.

CHAPTER SEVENTEEN

THE RESTAURANT WAS in the middle of nowhere. It felt to Sarah as if they'd driven down every tiny country lane in the area. She sat in the back of the car as Amir chatted about business, their friends in the city, and some of the conversations he'd had regarding the wedding.

"My mother summoned me for a long talk," he said.

Sarah blanched. Claudette was a force to be reckoned with and she had no doubt the conversation had been one-sided, with Claudette telling Amir exactly what she thought of Sarah.

"I assured her everything was okay between us and I promised her a beautiful wedding soon." He smiled and squeezed Sarah's leg. "She was starting to doubt you."

Sarah squeezed Amir's leg back and offered her own half-hearted smile. She needed to tell Amir about her own doubts, but she didn't want to do it in front of Jacques.

Amir turned away and stared out the window at the passing scenery. "Your running away like that made her wonder." His voice was cool.

"I didn't run away," Sarah said, which she knew wasn't quite the truth.

"No," Amir said. "That's just what I told her."

Sarah wasn't sure he was entirely convinced.

Up in front, Jacques was his usual silent model of discretion. Even so, she'd never become comfortable with holding personal conversations in his presence. She knew nothing about Jacques's private life, other than he had once been a bodyguard for a famous rock star who'd succumbed to a lethal combination of sex, drugs, and rock and roll. The aging star had allegedly come briefly out of retirement for a comeback tour, taken up, as was customary, with a young groupie, but had got carried away, forgotten to take his heart medicine and suffered a massive coronary while eating his morning prunes. As a consequence, Jacques had found himself suddenly and unexpectedly unemployed. He'd been Claudette's personal driver ever since, and she refused to be chauffeured by anyone else. Which was what made Sarah suspicious about him driving Amir now. She wouldn't put it past Claudette to have sent Jacques as a spy. She wasn't going to say another word until they were alone. Even then, she knew she'd have to guard her true feelings about the woman who was supposed to become her mother-in-law.

Jacques finally turned down a lane so narrow that Sarah had no idea what would happen if something came the opposite direction. He pulled the Jaguar into a small gravel car park and stepped out to open the door for Sarah. Amir appeared at her other side the second her foot touched the ground. He took her arm and escorted her inside. There weren't many cars parked outside and Sarah thought that seemed like a bad sign for a Saturday night, but when they stepped inside the restaurant she saw why.

The room was small and impeccably decorated in a French bistro style, with tiled floors and rich yellow walls. Scattered around the space, tucked into alcoves and window coves were a handful of round tables of two and four. A maître d' strode toward them, his hand outstretched. "Mr. Hillingham, a pleasure to see you again, Sir."

Again? When had Amir been here?

"Tony, you never age," said Amir, shaking the man's hand. "My mother sends her regards."

"She is well?"

"Indestructible." Amir laughed amicably and turned to Sarah. "This is my fiancée, Sarah Tildon."

Sarah reached out for a handshake, wondering how Amir knew a restauranteur two hundred miles from London, but Tony, in one deft movement, took her hand and lifted it toward him, placing the other hand on top and bowing has head. "Enchanté, Miss Tildon."

Tony led them to a table nestled beneath the main window. The sun was beginning to drop toward the horizon casting a warm, pink light over the valley below. It truly was breathtaking countryside and Sarah took in the rolling fields, the swath of woodland folding down to the river that wound its way through the valley like a stretch of gold ribbon.

Tony handed her a menu and shook out a black napkin, draping it across her lap. She watched as Amir closed the wine menu and held a short, whispered discussion with Tony, who nodded and hurried away. For the first time since she'd spotted Amir's car winding into the village they were alone.

"This is a lovely surprise," said Sarah.

"I hope so," Amir said. "I was surprised to learn you hadn't checked in at Atherton."

"I'm sorry," Sarah said, sensing an apology was expected.

Amir tilted his smooth chin, as if waiting for more of an explanation, but Sarah didn't feel like explaining.

"Anyway, it worked out fine," she said. "I've enjoyed the B&B and they've taken excellent care of me."

"But not your bike."

"That wasn't their fault."

"You loved that bike, or at least I thought you did."

"I do."

"And yet you lost it."

"To be fair, it was stolen."

Amir raised an eyebrow to say he felt differently about the matter. "It's not like you to be so careless with the things you care about."

Sarah looked away, feeling chastised. She broke the crust off a slice of fresh baguette and smeared it with a blob of dip. It tasted like heaven, but the bread caught in her throat. Amir knew all about her family history and she'd told him about the bike she'd loved and been forced to give back when they left. He was right that Sarah took care of the things she loved because of that, but she got the feeling Amir wasn't talking about the bike now.

"I just want the best for you," he said.

"I know," she said, "but sometimes I need to take care of myself."

"And rough it?"

Sarah laughed. "I've hardly been roughing it."

He reached out and took her hand, straightening the engagement ring that had spun around on her slender finger. From the look of the menu that sat in front of her, she was going to remedy that tonight.

"Your hands," he said. "They're so rough. What have you been doing?"

Sarah's mind flitted to Michael. Well, not to Michael exactly, but to his garden, to pulling up beets and planting peas. Her hands had been in the dirt, taking seeds and placing them where they could grow and become food. She'd been connecting with the earth. That sounded so hippyish, but it was true. For the past few days she'd felt as if she was a part of something bigger than herself and she'd belonged. She shook her head. There was something about this environment that brought out the romantic fool in her. If she told Amir any of this, he'd think she'd really lost her mind. Maybe he'd be the one to call off the wedding then. "It's just from riding, being outdoors, dehydrated." She was waffling. "And I haven't had a manicure in weeks."

Amir laughed. "I knew you'd been roughing it. Come on, let's order. You probably haven't had a proper meal since you left."

She thought about the breakfast Michael had made for her that morning, how she'd sat at his rough-hewn kitchen table, her knee tucked under her chin, drinking coffee and laughing. She blinked the image away, as if Amir might see it.

They perused the menu and took recommendations from their waiter, a small, lean man who seemed to swoop in and out like a spirit, anticipating their needs. They drank French champagne and ate escargot served with a decadent drizzle of melted butter, garlic, and parsley. The waiter brought salad with hearts of palm and sprinkled with local cheese. When the main courses arrived, the chef himself brought them out. He introduced himself to Amir, offering a fist bump, rather than an unsanitary handshake. He beamed at Sarah and told her about the vegetable terrine he'd created especially for her. She circled her nose above it and pronounced that it smelled delicious. The chef offered a deep bow of gratitude and strode back to his kitchen. Amir lifted his glass of Sancerre and waited for Sarah to do the same. "To an evening with my favorite person," he said and clinked his glass gently against Sarah's.

They ate in silence, each savoring the food, but Sarah's mind was tumbling with thoughts. This was a lovely surprise and spending the evening like this with Amir felt normal, like her real life. It was a good life and the short time she'd spent away from it made her appreciate it all the more. But she knew Amir. This wouldn't be a goodwill gesture. Not that he wasn't capable of random acts of kindness; he was. But he hadn't traveled halfway up the country, made arrangements for her bag, called ahead to request a special order from the chef in an exclusive restaurant, for the sake of a surprise. He would have come with an agenda, a desired outcome, and Sarah was fairly sure it had to do with the wedding.

"It rained here last Saturday," she said, prodding the conversation. "Did it rain at home?"

"We had a torrential downpour at two o'clock. I know because I was thinking about when it started and wondering if you had been caught in it."

"I had, but it arrived a little earlier here. By two o'clock I was already soaked."

"You know how to have fun." He laughed. "Perhaps it was a sign."

Sarah looked up from her meal, trying to gauge what he was saying. "A sign?"

"That we were right to move the wedding."

The thought had crossed Sarah's mind, although she'd seen it a little differently. She'd seen it as an omen that the planned wedding would have been rained out if it had taken place. She couldn't help but admit to herself too, that if she'd had the wedding she'd really wanted, the simple country wedding, the simple *outdoor* country wedding, that she and Amir would have had to swim down the aisle as husband and wife.

"We could have saved money on the band at the reception and had mud wrestling for entertainment," she said.

"I think my mother may have excused herself early."

Sarah resisted the urge to say that would have made the day ideal as far as she was concerned. She'd made a pledge to herself to stay on her future mother-in-law's good side and Amir wouldn't tolerate a bad word said against the family matriarch.

"Have you been thinking about the new plans while you've been riding?"

"A little," she said. "To be honest, I've been enjoying the quiet time alone. It's been a stressful couple of months. Thank you for being flexible with me."

Amir nodded in acknowledgement, but it was a small nod, not exactly a full endorsement of her decision. "And the wedding?"

Sarah hesitated. She was going to have to tell Amir about her doubts soon, but did she really want to do it here? "I'd expected to have a little more time to get my thoughts in order," she said.

"What's to think about? We just need to set a new date soon, put people's minds at ease."

"People like your mother?" she said.

"For one. But she's not the only one with, shall we say, concerns."

"Well, I don't care what people think. We know our reasons for canceling the wedding and if people want to read more into it than that, there's nothing I can do about it. Some people just love to gossip."

"Postponing," Amir said.

"Sorry?"

"Postponing the wedding. You said 'canceling'."

"Did I?"

Amir nodded.

Sarah held his gaze but her eye twitched with the strain of not looking away. "You know what I meant."

Amir didn't respond and Sarah got the feeling that he might be joining the list of people with doubts about the wedding.

"Dear Sarah," he said at last. "I'm not a fool. I don't know what's been going on here, but it's clear this place—or someone in it—has been playing tricks on you, a holiday romance of sorts. I know you like your freedom and I've done everything I can to give you space. But this isn't real life, Sarah. You, of all people know that dreams and fairy-tales don't keep a roof over your head."

Sarah put down her fork, no longer hungry. It was a low blow, but he was right. Her dad had been a dreamer, always scheming the next get-rich idea, and he hadn't been able to keep a roof over his family's heads. What Michael had was a fairytale life and she'd enjoyed the best bits of it.

But what when the winter came? What when the heating broke? What when the chickens stopped laying and the rabbits got to the lettuces and the potatoes got blight? And what about children? It wasn't fair to bring children into such an unstable life. It wasn't just about money—she could support herself—it was the lifestyle. She'd had enough adventure and uncertainty in her childhood and would never impose that on a child of her own. Amir was stable, solid, reliable. He came from a family with firm roots and a secure footing. And he was kind and thoughtful, generous and supportive. Surely that was enough. She was ready to settle down and Amir could give her the kind life she wanted. Couldn't he?

"I don't want to marry your mother," she said, not able to meet his gaze.

"I promise you," said Amir, "that once we are married, we can have the life we want."

"You keep saying that, but is it true?"

"I promise."

"But?"

"But we just need to give my mother the wedding she wants."

"And then?"

"And then I will give you the life you want."

As the sun slipped down behind the hill and the waiter brought their coffee, Sarah took a long look at the view. She loved it here, but Amir was right. He could give her what she really wanted, a stable foundation on which to build their life together. Her time with Michael had been fun, but he was a dreamer, just like her father, and she wasn't willing to risk her heart that way again.

CHAPTER EIGHTEEN

IT WAS dark by the time Michael stood up from the bike and stretched his back. He stepped back and admired his handiwork. He felt a momentary flinch of embarrassment. Even he had to admit The Contraption was not at all easy on the eyes. If he'd had more time, he would have repainted the frame, wrapped the handlebars in matching tape, polished up the components and cleaned up the saddle. But he didn't have time. Nicki was right; ever since Caroline had left, he'd been afraid to take risks. He'd played it safe. But he couldn't play it safe with Sarah. Because when he pictured the kind of life he wanted and the kind of person he wanted to share it with, he had always envisioned someone like Sarah. And if he didn't tell her before she left, he'd regret it for the rest of his life.

He turned off the barn light and locked the door behind him. As he made his way back to the farmhouse, he glanced down the lane to Sunnydale. There was a light on in Sarah's room. He hurried to the wall and peered down the lane. The midnight blue Jaguar was parked outside. She was back. His heart sank as he pictured her up in her room with this Amir person. Surely she wouldn't be so cruel as to sleep with him under Michael's own sister's roof?

The axe was still where he'd left it in the woodpile. For a moment he considered taking it to The Contraption, smashing it to smithereens the way Sarah had smashed his heart. But then he spotted a figure stepping through the gate of Sunnydale. A man. He was shorter and stockier than Michael had imagined from Nicki's description. And although he couldn't really see the man's features from this far away, his overall image wasn't what Michael would consider "devastatingly good-looking."

Just then the light in Sarah's room went out. The man climbed into the car, started the engine and drove away. Michael's heart skipped. Maybe he should go over there now and let her know he was there.

No, he told himself. He'd wait until the morning. He'd let her sleep on whatever had happened between her and her fiancé and tomorrow he'd take her the bike and tell her how he felt.

CHAPTER NINETEEN

SARAH'S THOUGHTS had been hopping all evening, trying to land on something concrete, but as Jacques maneuvered the car through the narrow lanes away from the restaurant, her mind flatlined. She had promised Amir a wedding date and there was nothing more to think about. She had stopped paying attention to their route long ago, but as the car slowed to a halt, she brought her attention back to Amir. As she peered out the window she was surprised to see they had stopped not outside Sunnydale, but Atherton Hall. She looked at Amir, questioningly.

"I'll give you all the space you need," he said, "but for God's sake, there's no need to rough it."

Sarah felt the objection rise up inside her. Sunnydale was hardly roughing it. She was comfortable there, relaxed. At home.

"Could you give us a moment, please, Jacques?" said Amir.

The chauffeur nodded and stepped out of the car. It felt suddenly very small in the back seat, almost too intimate for

Sarah. She knew that Amir had something important to say and she was pretty certain she knew what it was going to be. He was going to ask her to abandon her ride. That wouldn't be a problem, given that she had no bike. And then he was going to tell her it was time to come home, time to commit to the wedding, and time to stop making a fool of him. Or something like that, anyway.

"It was good to see you tonight," he said. "It made me realize how much I've missed you."

"I enjoyed it too," she said.

"Sarah?" His voice commanded her attention and she turned, but couldn't meet his eye, afraid of what she might see. "I love you, Sarah," he said. "And I want you to be my wife. But I also want you to *want* to be my wife."

"I do," she started to say, but he held up his hand to stop her.

"I want you to marry me for the right reasons and I want you to be sure. I wish you'd come home with me tonight and we can start making our plans, but we agreed on two weeks and I want you to take it. When you come home to be my wife, I want you to come prepared and ready, without doubts."

She nodded so he could see she had heard and understood.

She felt his hand under chin and he lifted her face up so she had no option but to look at him. All she could think about was kissing Michael in the middle of the stone circle, and the harder she tried to push the image aside, the more she was sure Amir could see her guilt.

"I want you to take this time," he said again. "But Sarah, I do want you to come home. I want you to marry me."

He smiled that smile that twanged at her heart. She felt something inside her melt. Then he leaned forward and kissed her tenderly on the cheek. The intensity caught her by surprise. This wasn't a kiss of someone who didn't care. It was the kiss of a man who loved her.

"Are you...?" she hesitated. "Are you coming in?" Even as she said it she wasn't sure she should have. She wanted to be alone. He'd given her the time to think and she wanted to take it.

"No," he said. "I need to get back to the city and you need your sleep." He kissed her again and, as if by magic, Jacques opened the door. "Goodnight," Amir said.

"Goodnight."

Jacques walked her to the reception and rang the bell. When she glanced back to the car, Amir's face was lit by the glow of his cellphone screen. He was already working again. Sarah felt piqued that he hadn't walked her in, didn't even seem that interested in her.

From the wall behind the reception desk, Claudette peered down from her portrait.

"Jacques," Sarah said, tentatively. "Claudette sent Amir to get me, didn't she?"

"Not at all," Jacques said. "It was Mr. Hillingham's idea to come."

Sarah exhaled, relieved that Amir had come under his own steam.

"Still, Mrs. Hillingham always gets her way," Jacques said.

Sarah snapped her head around to look at him, trying to gauge what he meant. Before she could ask, Guillaume appeared, gushing greetings and ushering her up the stairs, and Jacques was already at the main doors. She called goodnight to Jacques but he was already gone. She let Guillaume guide her to her room, wondering what Jacques had meant.

She wasn't surprised when Guillaume opened the door

to her room and let her in to find her panniers and bag sitting on the fold-out luggage rack. Jacques must have been dispatched to Sunnydale to collect her bags and wrap up her account while she and Amir were at dinner. Amir, snapping his fingers and making magic happen again. She wished she'd had the chance to say goodbye to Nicki and to thank her for her hospitality. She wished she'd been able to see Michael, too. But what would she say?

When she closed the door behind her, she sensed immediately that there was something out of place in the room. The covers had been turned down and a single peach rose had been laid on her pillow. Under Amir's orders, no doubt. He would never do anything so pedestrian as to leave a red rose. She kicked off the high heels, her tired feet glad to be able to stretch out again, and picked up the rose. There was a tag tied to the stem with a cream-colored ribbon. Sarah recognized Amir's elegant swooping handwriting.

My Sarah,

Finish what you started. Don't give up on something so good.

All my love,

Amir.

Well, that wasn't a note from a disinterested man, even if his choice of words wasn't the most romantic. "Finish what you started." It made their relationship sound like a DIY project, like "now you've built this thing, don't forget to sand it down and paint it." Still, it meant he wanted her. She plopped onto the bed, still holding the rose and the note.

Something caught her eye.

Behind the door, where it would have been hidden when she came in, was Cecelia. She stood there, gleaming like new, a peach bow attached to the drop handle bars. Sarah hadn't expected to see her ever again. She assumed she would have been stripped down and the parts sold off for a tidy profit, but there she was, complete. She moved toward Cecelia and ran her hand over the white frame and the soft, spongy curves of her handlebar wraps. She caressed the seat that had carried her all this way, and admired the gleaming set of gears. Whoever had done the work to clean up Cecelia had done an impeccable job. They'd even repaired the chips of paint from the seat stem.

She looked again. There was no evidence that any damage had ever been done. The tires showed no sign of wear and when she peered at the gear wheels she could see that they'd never turned a single rotation in their short lives. She ran her hand over the handlebars again. No lamb bell. No sign it had ever been there. Amir hadn't recovered Cecelia; he'd replaced it.

She did a quick check of all the custom components she'd added over the years. Every single one was there, exactly as she'd built it. It had taken her about five years to build the bike of her dreams, to learn which components suited her best, and to buy them one by one whenever she had the extra cash. She estimated she'd spent several thousand pounds building Cecelia. Amir had researched, purchased, and had a duplicate assembled in the space of two days. She was thrilled to have her bike back, or a version of it, but it left her feeling somehow hollow. Cecelia had been her pride and joy, the most valuable thing that she had ever owned, but it wasn't just the price that made her valuable. It was so much more complicated than that. It was the history, the adventures, the stories behind each part she'd added, the experience of learning about her sport. It was the pride she felt in building Cecelia herself, knowing that she'd worked hard and paid for it. Cecelia was *her* bike, truly hers. And the fact that Amir had replaced her so easily felt wrong.

She shook off the thought. How ungrateful could she be? Of all the surprises he could have given her tonight—and there were some that would have come as no surprise at all—this was above and beyond anything she could have imagined. He hadn't just given her a (very) expensive bike; he'd given her ultimate freedom. He'd given her the ability to finish the ride she'd started, the freedom to take her time thinking about their relationship, the chance to decide she wanted something else, if that's the conclusion she came to. He had given her the opportunity to decide her own future. It was the most valuable gift she could have asked for.

She realized then that she'd never heard the car pull away. She hurried to the window and peered through a gap in the curtain to the forecourt below. The car was still there, with Amir leaning against it. He hadn't been engrossed in his phone at all; it had all been part of his surprise. She felt a surge of affection inside her for this wonderful, thoughtful man. He gave her so much and really, he asked so little in return. She would have to be a complete idiot not to marry him. Complete and utter idiot, the most foolish woman in the history of foolish women.

Amir glanced up and smiled. She waved to him, wondering if she should go down to say thank you, to ask him to stay the night after all, maybe even suggest they borrow a bike so he could finish the ride with her. But before she could move, he waved and climbed into the car. The door closed and Jacques eased the car away.

Finish what you started. Don't give up on something so good.

Sarah smiled, grateful that he understood how important this trip was to her. But a little place at the bottom of her heart ached for his company. It was a lonely little spot.

CHAPTER TWENTY

MICHAEL WAS UP SO EARLY the next morning the chickens were barely awake when he went out to feed them. They grumbled in their roosts and clucked their disapproval at being disturbed, but none of them could be bothered to stir.

"Big day, ladies." Michael tipped feed into their tray. "Preen those feathers so you look good, okay?"

The chickens clucked and went back to sleep.

Michael checked the egg trays. Three eggs. He huffed at the chickens. Was it Caroline's call that had upset them? Or was it Sarah's absence? He mustered his resolve to get her back, for his chickens and for himself.

In the barn, Michael gave The Contraption a last dust down and wheeled it over to Sunnydale. It was quiet in the village. The milkman was making his rounds and old Mrs. Belmont was out for her walk, limping slightly on her bad hip. At the end of the village, a white van backed out into the street and headed his way. It slowed as it reached him, and the driver rolled down the window.

"What the bloody hell is that contraption?" Jamie said, eying the bike.

"A present," Michael said.

Jamie raised his eyebrows but he gave Michael a sly look. "Flowers and chocolates are more traditional, you know."

"Not for Sarah."

Jamie frowned. "Not being funny, mate, but didn't I see her leave in a Jag last night?"

"You did."

Jamie gave him a questioning look.

Michael grimaced. "A glitch, I know. Which is why I'm going over there now to sort it out."

Jamie held up his hand. "It's not that. I've seen that car here before. Last week. Don't know who this guy is, but I'd watch my back if I were you."

Michael hesitated. Sarah's fiancé had been in the village before? Was he spying on her? That would be creepy.

"Good luck, my friend," Jamie said as he rolled up the window and drove away.

I don't need luck, Michael thought. But his stomach tickled with anticipation and just the tiniest bit of worry for Sarah.

He ducked down the lane that ran behind Sunnydale and went in through the back gate. He could already smell bacon and homemade muffins wafting from the kitchen. His stomach growled. He shut the gate behind him, not wanting to risk another bike to opportunistic thieves. He straightened the bow he'd tied to the handlebars, patted down the collar of his denim shirt, and stepped into the bustle of the kitchen.

Nicki was at the stove, juggling three different pans. Jennie was feeding bread into the toaster with one hand and operating the coffee maker with the other. They both looked focused on their work. Both stopped when Michael stepped in.

Right at that moment, he knew something was wrong.

"Sit," said Nicki. She laid three strips of bacon, a fried egg, and a heap of mushrooms on a plate and handed it to him. Jennie swooped in with a mug of coffee and two slices of toast. Nicki dished up the food she was cooking and Jennie hurried out into the breakfast room to serve it.

"Eat," Nicki said.

"I'm not hungry," Michael said.

"Eat anyway."

"She left, didn't she?"

His sister nodded. "Last night. The driver came and picked up her things, settled the bill, and left."

Michael's chest slumped. It wasn't Amir he'd seen the night before, but his driver, dispatched to collect Sarah's belongings. "Did he say where she'd gone?"

Nicki shook her head.

"You know, I just saw Jamie. He thinks he saw that car here last week. Do you think her fiancé had her followed?" Michael said, and immediately realized how stupid he sounded.

Jennie came back in and slid an order onto the rack. Nicki glanced at it and dropped two eggs into the hot pan. A look passed between the two of them and Michael knew they'd already talked about what had happened.

"I've got work to do," Michael said, the first excuse he could think of.

Nicki nodded to Jennie to take over at the stove and she slid into the chair next to him and rested her hand on his. "I'm really sorry," she said.

"She didn't even say goodbye." He'd been stupid to even

think there was anything between them. She was just a tourist, someone passing through, someone who happened to be attractive—okay, happened to be very attractive—and someone who, in another time, a time when maybe he'd been looking for a mate and a time when she didn't already have one, that maybe, just maybe, there could have been something there.

"It just wasn't meant to be," Nicki said.

Michael grunted. He hated when Nicki got philosophical.

"I know you don't want to hear this," she said, "but there's more than one someone for everyone. The world is too big and too chaotic for there to be only one perfect match for each of us."

"You got that from Mum," he said. Their mother was always pragmatic when it came to love. She'd say, "What if your someone lives on the opposite side of the world, or in a remote Amazonian village?" Her philosophy was that it didn't make any sense that humans, creatures who thrived on intimate personal relationships, could have only one perfect match and such an infinitesimal chance of connecting. His mother always told him that there would be plenty of perfect matches for him throughout his lifetime, and they were a lot like buses: Sometimes one wouldn't come along for ages, and then three would come all at the same time. The trick with it, she told him, was not to be greedy, but to be satisfied with enjoying the person you were with, for all her traits, and not to constantly compare and look for something better. Pity Caroline's mother hadn't instilled that in her daughter.

Because no one was perfect, his mother said, and every relationship took some compromise. But even his mother would have said that a giant engagement ring was too big an obstacle to work around. "It wasn't meant to be," his mother would have said. "Maybe in another time and place it could have been wonderful, but it's here and now and so you have to let it go."

The chickens were awake when Michael got back. He felt around in their laying trays and came up with three more eggs. He needed Sarah to sing to them. That alone should be reason for her to come back.

But she wasn't coming back. The sooner he and the chickens accepted that, the better off they'd all be.

Michael sat on the floor of the chicken coop and began to sing. It was a mournful song of heartbreak and loss, so pitiful that even the chickens scurried out of the coop away from his misery.

What a complete idiot he was. Not just about Sarah, not just about the ramshackle bike, but about everything. What kind of idiot gave up a life in the city and fooled himself into thinking he could make a life in the country from the sweat off his own back.

"This kind of idiot," he said. But no one was left to hear him.

CHAPTER TWENTY-ONE

JUST ONE WEEK after The Wedding that Wasn't, Sarah lay in the spa room of Atherton Hall, cocooned in white blankets, her eyelids held closed by two cool circles of cucumber. Every breath she took was filled with a gentle lavender aroma and the only sound she could hear was the haunting cries of the Andean pipe music that wafted in through the sound system. This was as close to Nirvana as she could imagine. And still, her mind wouldn't shut up.

You don't belong here, it kept telling her. You don't belong.

She'd been hearing this same thought in her head her whole life, always feeling like she wasn't good enough to be anywhere nice, always worried someone would find out who she really was. She'd learned to silence the voice over the years, but now its meaning was different. It wasn't so much that she wasn't good enough to be here, just that she belonged somewhere else.

Her thoughts turned again to Michael. What would he be doing now? Singing to the chickens? Planting his pota- toes? Turning over his compost heap? She imagined the sun on her skin as she worked beside him, pictured them breaking for lunch and collapsing in an exhausted heap on his lumpy couch, imagined them at the end of the day, fatigued from a day of labor, flushed from hot showers, tucking into a homemade meal and homegrown vegetables, rolling into bed together and sleeping that beautiful blissful sleep that can only come after being outdoors.

She never slept that way in London, always aware of the bustle of the city, the Tube rumbling beneath her, sirens wailing into the night. The city never stopped moving and it made it hard to truly rest. In Hope she'd had the best sleep of her life.

In London, though, she had security. She had to be honest with herself. She couldn't live the life Michael lived. On her first day in Hope he'd been worried because his chickens had stopped laying. What if his crops failed or the weather turned against him or the hot water heater broke and he couldn't afford to fix it? She'd grown up with the uncertainty of not knowing where her next meal would come from and she didn't want to live that way again. She had a good life and she'd be crazy to give it up. She should just go home and make everything right with Amir. "The ring doesn't make the marriage," her mother had told her, and nor did the wedding. She would give Claudette the wedding she wanted, then get on with her marriage and life with Amir.

So why, now that she had come to her senses about going back to her real life, did she feel so empty?

A high-pitched chime of Tibetan tingsha bells roused Sarah from her thoughts. Someone lifted the cucumber circles from her eyes and a young woman with ice-blonde hair pulled tight to her scalp peered down at her. "Ready for your manicure, Miss Tildon?"

Sarah was not ready for her manicure. She felt itchy in her skin, like she needed to run away from herself. What she wanted was to get on her new bike, and pedal until her thoughts fell into place. Instead, she said, "Okay," and let the manicurist lead her to yet another room.

At least this one had a window. Sarah sank into the deep white chair and let the mechanism lift her legs and tilt her backwards until she was looking at the sky at the top of the window. It was a beautiful day, little puffy clouds floating by and birds swooping in the sunlight and perching in a nearby tree. She wished she could feel the breeze on her face.

The manicurist's hands were cold, like tiny icicles pressed against Sarah's warmed skin. "Goodness me," she said. "What have you been doing with your nails?"

Sarah glanced at her hands. The skin was callused across her palms from holding a trowel. She had a line across her fingers and a tan circle on the back of her hands where her cycling gloves had been. Her cuticles were ragged and her nails split and jagged. In the crease where her nail overhung the nail bed, thin half-moons of dirt were wedged in. No amount of scrubbing had been able to shift them.

"You have farmer's hands," said the woman, smiling sweetly, although Sarah could see she was not impressed. "I'm going to do a mask for them. I'll just be a moment."

Sarah heard the door open and she let her eyelids drift closed. Her thoughts swooped like the birds outside. They wheeled to her hands in the dirt, flitted over her new bike, and came to land on the contraption Michael had shown her that night. It was such an odd machine, pieced together with bits of other people's leftovers, second-hand cast-offs.

And yet the thought of it stopped her breath. He had made that for her, with his own hands, with love.

The door opened and Sarah pushed all thoughts of Michael and the contraption from her mind.

"You looked relaxed," a cool voice said.

Sarah tensed. Her eyes flew open and there, peering down at her with a haughty smile, was her mother-in-law-to-be. "Claudette. This is a surprise."

"I came to check on the flood damage. I hope you're enjoying your stay," Claudette said.

"It's lovely," said Sarah. It was the truth, or it had been until Claudette had arrived. It was a bit of a coincidence that Claudette had chosen this occasion to visit a property herself instead of sending one of her minions.

"Amir was glad to see you last night. He said Tony pulled out all the stops for you."

"It was lovely," Sarah said, wondering if this is all she would ever be able to say again.

"And did you like your gift?"

"It's lovely."

"Although why on Earth you didn't tell us right away that your bike had been stolen, I'll never know."

Sarah opened her mouth to say that she hadn't wanted to bother Amir, but Claudette wasn't looking for an answer.

"Anyway, I'm glad you and Amir came to an agreement. But now I think it's time you took his feelings into consideration. You embarrassed my son, Sarah. And I don't like that. You need to come home and show him—and everyone else —how you feel."

"I—."

"I have some business to attend to, but Jacques will be waiting to drive us back when I'm finished. Please call my son and tell him you'll be home for dinner this evening."

And with that, Claudette turned on her patent leather heels and strode out.

Rage burned in the pit of Sarah's stomach. How dare that woman order her around? She and Amir had discussed that she would finish the ride and now Claudette was interfering again. Oh, she would call Amir all right. She would call him right now and tell him about his meddlesome mother.

She sat up in the chair.

Her phone!

Her mind flashed back to the last place she'd seen her phone. With Amir's arrival and all the events of the day, she had completely forgotten about her phone. She'd meant to call Nicki from her room and get a message to Michael, but now, with Claudette stalking around, she couldn't risk it.

"Let's take care of those hands for you, shall we?" The manicurist was back.

"No," said Sarah, pulling her hand away.

The manicurist stared at her like she had a madwoman on her hands.

"I'm sorry," Sarah said. "I'm not feeling too well. I think it's the heat from the body wrap."

"Too much champagne maybe?" said the woman, slyly.

"Perhaps that's it. I should lie down. I'm sorry, I'll have to do this another time."

"We're very busy," the manicurist called out to her, but Sarah was already out the door.

She ran down the hall from the spa, her thin Terry slippers almost tripping her. She kicked them off and ran up the two flights of stairs to her room. Before the door had even closed behind her, she shed her robe, grabbed an expensive-looking white towel, and wiped the layers of moisturizer and toning mask and goodness knows what other kinds of goop from her face.

Five minutes later, she was dressed in her bike gear, clipping into her pedals as the wheels of her bike spat out pebbles from the driveway behind her. She noticed the midnight blue Jaguar parked along the side of the building. But she didn't care if Claudette or Jacques saw her go. She had to get her phone now. And she had to clear her head.

CHAPTER TWENTY-TWO

MICHAEL DIDN'T BELIEVE in cosmic connections, but when the skin across his back prickled and *Sarah* popped into his head, he stood up from the strawberries he was tending and looked out to the lane. It was empty.

"Idiot," he said to himself and brushed his hands down his jeans. He needed to snap out of this. He didn't have time to indulge in self-pity; he had work to do. He collected his tools and moved to the next task on his long list of things to do. He pushed aside the thought that an extra set of hands would save the day.

"Need a hand?"

He looked up to where the voice had come from. And there was Sarah. She had a bike helmet clipped under her chin and was dressed in tight cycling clothes that high-lighted her best features, which in Michael's book was all of her. She leaned against a gleaming white bicycle. Michael's heart sank as he thought about the embarrassing contraption he'd almost presented her with.

"I thought you'd moved on," he said, trying to keep the bitterness out of his voice.

She didn't answer at first. "My plans changed unexpectedly," she said. She couldn't even meet his gaze and tell him straight up that her fiancé had showed up and that whatever had happened between them was in the past. "I just came for my phone. And to thank you."

"For what?"

She looked away. "For all your help with the calling tree."

He nodded. The calling tree hadn't helped to find Cecelia, but it had helped to build The Contraption. He looked at the gleaming machine leaning against her leg. "Looks like you didn't need it, after all."

Sarah looked away. "Anyway, I'm glad I got to know you... and your family. You're lucky to live in a place like this."

"Seems you have your own brand of luck," he said, indicating the bike.

Sarah's face colored. He didn't want to hurt or embarrass her, but what was he supposed to do? Just let her go?

"Look," she said, "I'm sorry I left when I did. I didn't have much choice."

"You have every choice. No one should be able to tell you what to do."

"It's not like that."

"Isn't it? What is it like then?"

She shook her head as if she was trying to find the right words. He wasn't about to offer them to her. She spoke. "What you're doing here is amazing. It's so brave and I really admire you. But I could never live like this."

Michael kicked at a clod of dirt by his toe. "Funny," he said, "you seemed to enjoy it for a while."

"I did," she said. She looked him dead in the eye then. "All of it."

He held her gaze. "I've always believed that life, even the hard stuff, is an adventure if you do it with the right person."

"That's what someone who's never had a hard life would say. You have this house, your family close by, a support system for the hard times. You don't know what it's like to be uprooted every year, never live in one place, have no one to rely on but yourself."

"So you're opting for security instead of love."

"Amir loves me."

He held up his hand in apology. "You're choosing safety instead of adventure."

She nodded.

"And here's me thinking you were the fearless type."

"I'm not," she said. "Not really."

"Well, the chickens will miss you. They like your singing better than mine."

She smiled. "Maybe I can send you a recording for them."

He shook his head. "They prefer the real thing."

For a moment, their eyes met and he was sure she was going to change her mind, stay for the sake of the chickens. But then she said, "I should go."

He nodded. "I'll get your phone."

He strode into the house, trying to keep his legs from wobbling. One half of him said he should turn around and run back to her, sweep her up in his arms and beg her to stay. The other half told him not to make a bigger fool of himself than he already had.

Upstairs, he found Sarah's phone on his dresser, just where she'd left it. He picked it up, catching the button on the side with his thumb. The screen lit up and Michael glanced at the notifications. Text from Amir. Call from

Amir. Six texts from Amir. Call from Amir. Michael tapped the button again and the screen went dark.

"Enough, Michael," he said out loud. It was time to let Sarah go. Back to her fiancé. Back where she belonged.

He couldn't look at Sarah as he walked back to hand her the phone. They shook hands, like they'd just negotiated an amicable ending to a business deal. Her cycling gloves left only the ends of her fingers exposed, but Michael relished the touch of her skin against his hand. He wished he could run his fingers over her palm, take her fingertips, touch them to his lips. Instead, he said, "Safe travels."

As she mounted her bike and clipped in, his aching heart told him to turn around and get back to work, back to the business of his life. But his feet wouldn't move. He watched her ride away, resisting the urge to call after her and beg her to come back. She lifted her arm at the end of the lane and waved. Before he could wave back, she was gone.

He wasn't sure how long he stood there, watching the spot where he'd last seen her, before a shadow fell across the wall in front of him and Nicki came into his line of sight.

"She's gone," he said. He looked to his sister, expecting sympathy, but her face was stern.

"And you let her?"

"She doesn't want to be here."

"Yes she does. She just doesn't know how to. You'll have to show her."

"It's too late."

Nicki put her hand on her hip and pursed her lips at him. "You have a bike don't you?"

He was about to shake his head when he remembered The Contraption. "I do."

"So go after her."

He stared at his sister, his mind racing over every interaction with Sarah. Her willingness to ride the Ferris wheel with Maddie and George, the chickens clucking as she sang to them, the sleepy look she had in the morning, the way she dug in and helped him. Most of all, he thought about how stiff and uncertain she looked this morning, and how utterly at home she'd looked in his house.

"I can't," he said.

Nicki threw up her hands. "Then I don't know what else to say."

"You all right, mate?" Jamie's van drew up by the wall and he leaned out, peering at Michael.

"Not all right," Nicki said.

"What's this idiot doing?" Jamie said.

"Thanks for the sympathy," Michael said, but when he looked up, Jamie wasn't looking at him. He was looking at a dark car that had pulled over on the wrong side of the road, blocking Jamie's van. It was a midnight blue Jaguar.

The driver's side door opened and the stocky man Michael had seen the night before climbed out. Amir's driver. What was he doing here?

"Has Miss Tildon been here?" he asked.

Michael flinched. So the fiancé *was* having her followed. What a creep. "You just missed her. Not much of a spy, are you?"

"Weren't you here last week?" Jamie asked. "I saw your car."

The man ignored Jamie and headed for Michael, reaching out to hand him something. "I found this."

He dropped something cool into Michael's palm. It was a bell, the kind a child would have on a bicycle. It was dappled with rust, a faded picture peeling from the top.

Michael peered at the image of an animal. Pale. A lamb. It was Sarah's missing bike bell.

"Where did you find this?"

"Perhaps you could return it to Miss Tildon?" The driver raise one eyebrow, like he and Michael were in on a secret.

"You *were* here last week," Jamie said. "That night her bike went missing."

Michael stared at the driver, but his expression gave nothing away.

"Was it you?" Michael asked. "Did you take her bike?" Even as he spoke the words, he couldn't believe they could be true. Sarah's fiancé had sent his chauffeur to steal her bike?

"I think perhaps Miss Tildon could explain it to you," the driver said, doing the eyebrow thing again.

The gears spun in Michael's head. How long had it been since Sarah had left? He'd never catch her on foot.

"Will you take me?" Michael asked.

The driver held up his hands. "Nothing to do with me," he said.

"You do have a bike," Nicki said, helpfully.

Michael stared at his sister. "This is insane."

"Then it's right up your alley."

He didn't wait for more encouragement. He clutched the bell in his hand and ran for The Contraption.

CHAPTER TWENTY-THREE

SARAH'S LEGS screamed as she reached the top of the hill. Her lungs burned and her breath rasped in her chest as she fought back the stupid tears that wouldn't stop. When she reached the summit she pulled over and leaned her bike against the wall, letting the tears finally have their moment. Of all the goodbyes she'd been through in her strange and transient life, this one had been among the worst. Saying goodbye to Michael was the right thing to do, she knew that. It didn't mean the right thing was the easy thing though. It rarely was. She gasped out a last sob and rubbed her eyes dry.

Now that she could see again, the view from up here was astounding. The rolling hills stretched out for miles in front of her. To the west, the ridge of a series of peaks punctuated the skyline. A river glistened in the valley below her as it wound its way steadily to the sea. There was a whole big beautiful world out there just waiting to be explored, a whole world of adventure with Amir.

Only he wasn't there, was he? He had given her the

freedom she wanted, this gorgeous bike and the time to enjoy it, but he had never wanted to come along for the ride.

Below her, the little village of Hope sat nestled in the valley, the late afternoon sun just grazing the top of the church spire. It was a lovely place, enchanting, and it had caught her up in its spell. She'd fallen for Nicki and her big laugh, Michael's family and their tight bond. And Michael himself and his crazy dream of a simpler life. Romance was fun but it didn't pay the rent, her mother had taught her that. Michael had been... what had he been? A stop gap? A momentary lapse in judgment? Her mother had married for love. How many times had she told Sarah that? And she'd paid the price for the rest of her life. No, Michael had been proof. He'd been proof that she couldn't trust herself. She was her father's daughter and she'd almost made the same mistake, almost thrown it all away for a silly fantasy. Sarah couldn't live like that. She wanted more from her life and Amir was the answer. She had to keep moving forward.

She allowed herself one last glance back at Hope before she lifted the bike from where it leaned against the wall and prepared to mount it again, prepared to head off into her future.

As she turned to check for traffic, she spotted a cyclist clawing his way up the hill, the bike moving so slowly, it looked like it might stop and topple over. The gears slipped with a clunk and the rider struggled to keep upright. That thing needs a tune-up, thought Sarah. But the rider persevered, using all the power of his legs to urge the bike up the hill. The rider finally looked up; it was Michael. He grinned at her briefly before gritting his teeth to make the last push to the summit.

Finally, he wobbled to a stop. His face glistened with

sweat and the damp hair around his temples sprung into tight shiny curls. "Caught. You." He gasped for breath.

"Michael," she said, determined to put a stop to all his nonsense once and for all. But he reached into his pocket and held out his hand. On his palm sat the silver lamb bell Grandma Lily had given her. "You found it." She could hardly believe it.

"A burly man in a fancy car gave it to me. He said you could explain it."

"Jacques?" Sarah said. "I don't understand."

She stared at Michael, trying to comprehend what he was saying. Jacques had found her bell? But how?

She ran back through the past day, trying to find some shred of a clue.

Jacques, the silent driver who saw and heard everything but seldom said a word. Jacques, who answered to Claudette's every whim. Jacques, who'd somehow managed to find the one single piece of Sarah's missing bike that she cared about the most. What had he told her the night before? "Mrs. Hillingham always gets her way."

"There's something I need to do," she said.

Michael nodded. "Will you come back?"

Sarah grinned. "Will you be here if I do?"

He took her hand and laid her fingers on his chest, right at the spot where his heart was thudding. "Right here," he said.

Back at Atherton Hall, Sarah showered and washed her hair, keeping her eye on the cool white tile until her heart rate slowed and her fury subsided. When she was dressed, she repacked the bag Amir had brought and folded her travel gear into her panniers. When she got downstairs, Jacques was waiting for her.

"Mrs. Hillingham isn't quite ready yet, Miss Tildon," he

said. "Perhaps I can take your luggage?"

Sarah didn't budge.

"Where's your bike?" Jacques asked.

Sarah held out her hand and showed him the bell. "I was hoping you could tell me."

Jacques's face was a mask. He didn't look surprised, didn't try to look ashamed. He simply nodded. He glanced quickly at the entrance and seeing the coast was clear, led Sarah around the side of Atherton Hall, through the secret garden, to a storage shed behind an ivy-clad wall. Inside was Cecelia, just as Sarah had last seen her in Nicki's shed, intact except for the little bell.

She handed her bag to Jacques. "You can take this to Mr. Hillingham. I'll call him and let him know you're coming. Oh, and please tell *Mrs.* Hillingham she won't be getting her dream wedding. In fact, she won't be getting any wedding at all."

Jacques nodded and took the bag from her. He didn't say a word.

"Oh, and Jacques?" He looked up. "Thank you for being a decent man. There aren't many like you left in the world."

Jacques smiled. "Just a few of us, Miss. I suspect you know another."

"I do," said Sarah and wheeled Cecelia out of the shed.

Out in the forecourt of Atherton Hall, she clipped on her panniers and fixed the silver bell to Cecelia's handlebar. "Back where you belong," she said.

She rolled up the leg of her cargo pants, slid into the familiar saddle, and pushed off down the driveway. She rang the bell once, a farewell to Atherton Hall. She didn't ring it again until she crossed the stone bridge and rode into Hope.

EPILOGUE

NICKI PINNED a yellow Gerbera daisy to the pocket of Michael's waistcoat and kissed him on the cheek.

"You clean up nicely," she said.

"What about me?" said Jamie.

"I don't have an opinion on you," Nicki said, "but Harry Belmont looks impressed."

Michael glanced out to where a small group of friends and neighbors from the village had shuffled into the rows of hay bale seats. He'd heard that Harry Belmont, Jamie's old flame, was visiting her gran, but he'd been so wrapped up in wedding preparations, he hadn't paid much attention.

"Ancient history," Jamie said, but Michael noticed the familiar wistful note in his friend's voice whenever Harry's name came up.

"History repeats," Michael said, but before Jamie could give any of his usual arguments about how he didn't want his heart broken again, the band struck up the first notes of *The Pushbike Song*. Michael's heart pounded in his chest. The sound grew louder as everyone fell silent. The crowd turned and Michael dabbed a drop of perspiration from his forehead. This was it.

~

FROM BEHIND THE CHICKEN COOP, Sarah pushed two little girls out into the field. The daughters of Sarah's colleagues from the wildlife rescue, they were dressed in simple cotton dresses and pale pink wellies. They scattered petals on the grass as they walked down the aisle between rows of folding chairs. Behind them went Maddie and George, grinning at their friends and neighbors.

The entire village had come out to watch the ceremony. A few friends had made the trip up from London and filled the rooms of Sunnydale and The White Swan. Sarah's brother Luke had been the first to respond that he wouldn't miss the wedding for anything. Nicki and Jamie had been working together for weeks to organize the reception food and coordinate with Michael as to what would be ready to harvest. Sarah had sung to the chickens every night to coax enough eggs from them for the cake. Maddie had given up being a cool tween and had been buzzing with excitement all week. And Michael... Sarah had pinched herself several times a day whenever she thought about Michael and their future together.

Sarah dusted down her simple pale dress that fell to her ankles in floating sheer fabric. Her hair was loose, just as Michael loved it, caught up at the sides and held with a simple wreath of flowers. She wore barely any make-up and she felt her skin glow with the radiance of someone who spent time outdoors. As she made her way toward Michael, all she could see was his smile, his beautiful big smile.

She took his hand and he squeezed it tight. "Fancy an adventure?" he asked.

Her smile softened and her eyelids fluttered closed for just a moment, as she pictured the life ahead of her, the hard work, the uncertainty, the simple life. And then she looked up and met his gaze. "I do."

STAY IN TOUCH

From time to time, I send Maggie Wild Love Letters with details on my new releases, special offers, and other goodies relating to the Hope Valley Romance series. You can stay in touch by signing up at: MaggieWild.com.

Enjoy this book? Share the love

Reviews are a powerful way to share books you love with other readers. And for authors, they're like little virtual hugs.

If you enjoyed this book, I would gratefully accept a hug (even a tiny one-sentence hug) in the form of a review of Amazon, Goodreads, or wherever you talk about books online.

Many thanks and big hugs back,
Maggie

Meet Harry and Jamie.

She's an independent go-getter who swore she'd never go home again. He's the beloved local chef who puts people before profits. When a serial cheater and a burned salmon dinner bring them together again, will their two old flames rekindle?

If you love feisty heroines, romantic dinners, and hopeful second-chances, then you'll adore Maggie Wild's fun tale of childhood sweethearts reunited.

ACKNOWLEDGEMENTS

I am grateful to all the people who encouraged and enabled me to write this book: Kathleen Guthrie Woods, Rayne Lacko, Nina Harrington, Teri Case, Maya Rushing Walker. Thank you to Megan Records for her keen editor's insight, and Eddy Bay for her sharp eye for detail. To Mum for providing a room of my own to write. And J for the care and feeding.

ABOUT MAGGIE

Maggie Wild lives in California Wine Country with her own Mr. Right and a small collection of furry friends. A native of Yorkshire, England, she visits "home" every day through her fictional worlds. When not writing her fun, contemporary romance stories, she loves to watch the birds in her garden and hike through the local redwoods.

Learn more at MaggieWild.com.

www.ingramcontent.com/pod-product-compliance
Lightning Source LLC
Chambersburg PA
CBHW021700110726
47902CB00007B/2001